The Wounded Nurse | Alex Amit

Printed in the United States of America

First Printing, 2022
Line Editing: Grace Michaeli

Contact: alex@authoralexamit.com
http://authoralexamit.com/

ISBN: 9798843729110

The Wounded Nurse

Part 1

Alex Amit

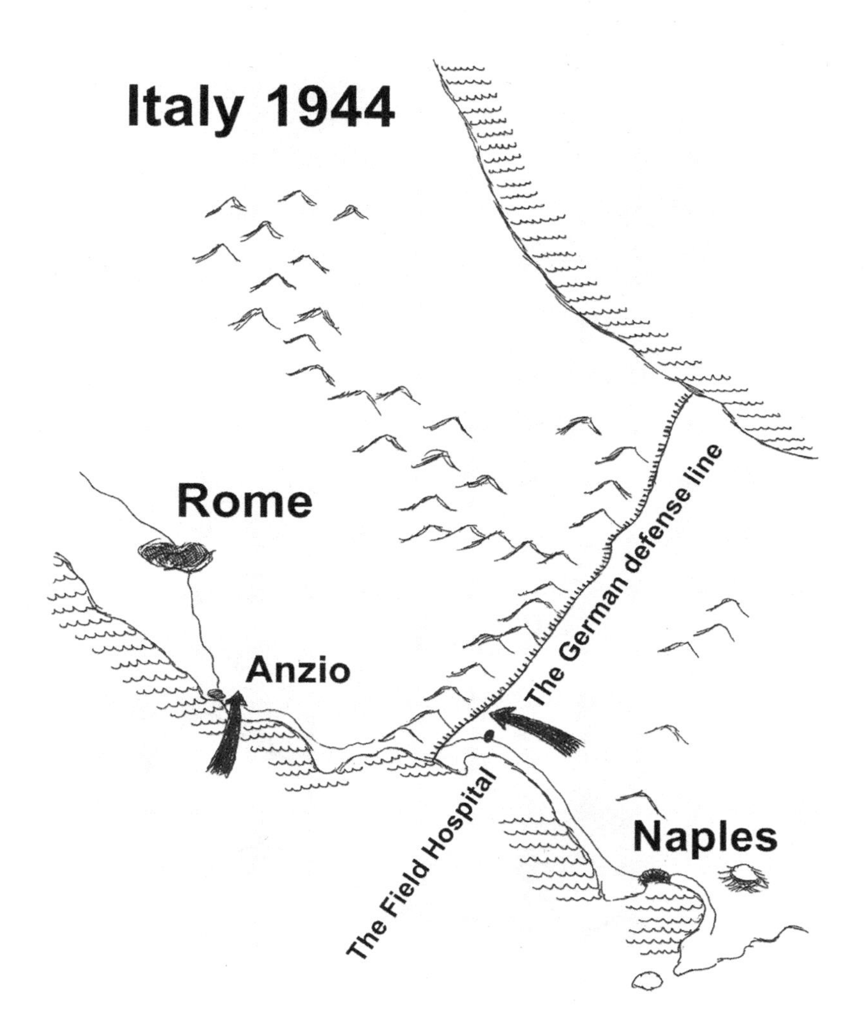
Italy 1944
Rome
Anzio
The German defense line
The Field Hospital
Naples

1. Italy, front line south of Rome, field hospital, April 1944.

"Are you the new nurse? Put your finger here," the doctor instructs me, and I press my fingers to the open wound in the chest of the wounded soldier as he lies on a stretcher placed in front of us on the simple wooden operating table.

"My name is Grace," I answer, ignoring my blood-soaked fingers as I try to stop the wounded man's bleeding as best I can.

"Vascular Scissors." He speaks quietly, and I collect them from the metal tray next to me, placing them in his hand. The tray is full of surgeons' chisels, sewing materials, and syringes. I must not make mistakes. Even though it was bright outside, it was was dark inside the tent, except for a dim yellow light from a lamp hanging from the tarp roof. It sways from side to side in the wind that shakes the tent sheets. In the weak light, I struggle to find the right spot to tack my fingers while the wounded soldier continues to bleed. I must succeed. The faint sound of raindrops that have been hitting the tarpaulin for three days interferes with my concentration. It is only disturbed by the sound of the scalpel blades or scissors I throw onto the stainless steel tray with sharp rings of metal. I can also hear the constant growl of cannon batteries firing in the distance, their muffled voices continuing unabated.

"Now try to take your finger off," the doctor instructs me after finding the point of injury and blocking it. I move my fingers away as he quickly stitches the exposed skin. "Cut another strip off his uniform and disinfect immediately afterwards."

I take my hands off the wound, hold the scissors, and quickly cut his torn uniform. It's soiled with mud and blood that have mixed together, until it's impossible to tell what's what. I throw the strips of cut cloth onto the muddy ground, then grab the bottle of alcohol and some cotton wool. I start cleaning the wounded soldier's skin, feeling his body shivering at the sting of disinfectant. I have to hurry, soon they'll be bringing in another wounded soldier. This one was also waiting to one side, lying in his stretcher, until we were finished taking care of the one before him.

I've lost count of the number of wounded soldiers I've treated in the last few days.

"How long have you been with us?" the doctor asks me.

"This is my fourth day." I stand proudly. I've hardly slept for the last three nights, working in this tent since I arrived at this hospital and the attack on the German lines began.

"The wound has reopened. Put your fingers on it again," the doctor speaks a little louder, and I toss the alcohol-soaked cotton swab and the scissors onto the metal tray, ignoring the jarring sound of metal hitting metal. My fingers are tucked into the open wound again, trying to stop the flow of blood staining the soldier's pale skin crimson.

"Where's another nurse?" He looks to the sides. "I need another nurse now, and two units of blood, stat."

"Nurse," I shout hoarsely, "we need two more units of blood now." My eyes are fixed on my wet fingers and the dripping stretcher full of blood. I can feel drops hitting my feet.

"Two units of blood on the table." Someone arrives and places two glass bottles filled with crimson liquid before disappearing in the direction of another operating tent. I have to get some rest.

"Now, to the vein, as you learned in nursing school," he tells me while my fingers are tucked inside the wound, and I feel the pulse through the throbbing artery and the pool of blood. "Do not take off his sleeve.

Cut it off." I turn my head towards the scissors thrown onto the metal tray. "Hurry up." His fingers replace mine.

"I can't find the vein," I whisper as I struggle with the needle, shoving it in over and over. I must succeed. He must live. I stop for a moment, wiping the sweat from my forehead and rubbing my eyes as I grab the wounded man's hand where it lies on the table, and try again.

"Good, now hold the bottle as high as you can, like you learned." He guides me as I find the wounded man's vein, and I lift the glass bottle high, ignoring my tired hands. Despite the cool breeze, I feel all sweaty; at least the rain has stopped, and the spring sun is shining between the tent sheets.

"Will he live?" I ask the doctor.

"I hope so." He smiles at me wearily. "What did you say your name was? Grace?"

"Yes."

"You're doing fine. Start binding his wound."

I carefully attach the blood bottle to the metal rod, and use the scissors to continue cutting off the wounded man's uniform, ignoring my tired and trembling hands. My fingers clean off the remaining blood with a cloth, and I disinfect his body again, opening a clean bandage and starting to cover his body.

"Is this okay?" I look at the doctor, who is leaning back and watching my hands.

"Yes, it's okay."

"Is this treatment tent three? I'm looking for the new nurse, Grace," I hear a male voice.

"That's me." I turn my gaze to the two uniformed soldiers entering the tent, carrying a stretcher with an unconscious, wounded man, placing him on the table at the side of the tent. One of the soldiers has a bandage on his forehead, and they're both dirty with dust and mud.

"We've brought you another two wounded, one with a chest injury and one with head and chest injuries."

The doctor approaches and looks at the wounded soldier, collects a stethoscope from the tray and checks his pulse.

"Take one of them. I can only treat one." He turns to the soldier with the bandage on his forehead and the Red Cross symbol on his arm.

"I can't. I was told to bring them both to tent number three, to ask for Grace. The rest of the operating tents are full," he says in a tired voice as two more soldiers enter, carrying another wounded man on a stretcher and placing it on the ground. The wounded man's eyes and chest are wrapped in bandages that were once white, and now are filled with ugly red spots. Since the attack began three days ago, they've been coming in an endless stream.

"Grace," the doctor instructs me, "take the one we treated to the recovery tent, and we'll start with that one," he points with his hand, "give him an injection of morphine."

"Help me carry him," I instruct the soldier while holding the wounded soldier as carefully as I can, and we both place him on the operating table. I need to rest, to get out of this suffocating tent, breathe some air that doesn't carry the smell of blood, and close my eyes for just a few minutes.

I go to the bucket of water standing to one side of the tent and dip my hands in the cold water, rinsing my face and eyes. I have to keep them open. My fingers grip the scissors again, and I start cutting the bandages covering the new wounded chest, ignoring his sigh of pain and the bloodstains on his once-khaki uniform.

In the distance I again hear the thunder of cannon batteries, getting louder, and maybe the howling of fighter plane engines, and a strange whistle accompanies the ticking noise of machineguns.

"Get down." I hear someone shouting, and I see round holes forming in the tent tarp. I reach my hand forward, trying to protect my face from shards of glass from the shattering lamp, or maybe it's the blood bottles hanging on the metal rod.

"What's happening?" I hear someone shouting, and maybe that's me who's screaming. I see the sheets of the tent being torn apart, and through the gray sky I see a huge flame at the spot where Surgical Tent Two had stood.

"German planes." someone yells from outside, and I pull the

wounded man from the operating table and carry him down into the mud, shouting at him that he'll be fine, but he doesn't answer me, and my ears are filled with the noise of drums until I can't hear my screams, or the screams of the people outside or around me in the tent, I don't know. It's just flames all around, and people are running, and maybe they're yelling too, and I grope on the muddy floor looking for the other wounded man who was in the tent, to pull them to the floor, but I can't see anything, mud or maybe blood is covering my eyes.

"They're shooting at us," I whisper, crawling on the floor, managing to find someone lying down, maybe one of the wounded from before, maybe it's the doctor. I'll clear the blood, and then I'll see.

"Don't worry, I'll protect you," I think I tell him as I lie down on top of him, but I'm not sure he's answered me. It's all flames, and the noise of aircraft engines and the constant ticking of machine guns, and my whole head is full of screams. I can't feel my leg, but it doesn't hurt at all.

"Don't worry, I'll take care of you," I whisper to him again, placing my head on his chest. I'll close my eyes for just a moment. Just a moment. "I'll take care of you."

***

2. Italy, a military hospital south of Rome, four months later, August 1944.

"Good morning, Grace, how are you this morning?" I hear Nurse Audrey, and feel her palm resting on my shoulder.

"Same as I'll feel tomorrow," I answer as I continue to lie on my white metal-framed bed, turning my back to her and looking at the yellow wall of what was once a magnificent mansion, now serving as a US Army hospital. My eyes examine the thin cracks in the plaster as if they were arteries bringing life to this place. But the plaster is peeling. Maybe this place should have died by now.

"How did you sleep?" She keeps talking to me, even though my gaze is turned to the yellow wall and I'm not looking at her. Maybe she should leave me here in the corner of the hall, and help the other wounded.

"Grace, sweetie, are you okay?" She strokes my shoulder.

"Like a corpse, I feel like a corpse," I answer. For four months now she's been asking me the same question, and for four months I've given her the same answer. But she still keeps coming every morning to take care of me, walking around my hospital bed in her white nurse uniform. I hate the white pajamas I wear, announcing who I am. Even prisoners are given unique uniforms, just in different colors and appropriate sizes. My pajamas are too big on me, and they're the smallest size they could find in this place. All the others around here are wounded male soldiers. I'm here by mistake. I'm a nurse who should be taking care of them instead of lying on this metal bed.

"Are you in pain?"

"Do you have anything to give me?" I keep staring at the wall. She's no longer willing to give me morphine. At first, when I was crying in pain, she would soothe me with a dose of morphine, coming to my bed at night and injecting me, and I would sigh in relief and manage to sleep. She's not willing to do that for me anymore.

"Don't you want to get out of bed?" I hear her bring my wooden crutches, placing them by my bed.

"Grace, you'll feel better if you get up and go out to the garden with the others in recovery."

"Do you think a missing leg can be recovered?" I whisper to the wall, hoping she doesn't hear me.

"At least you're alive," she answers, and pats me on the shoulder, continuing to talk to my back.

"Yes, at least I'm alive." I smile at the wall. Wall, do you hear? I survived, so it's okay to keep me in pain and not give me morphine when I ask for it. Maybe this whole staying alive thing was a mistake.

Only Audrey and the Italian cleaning woman come to my corner every morning. Audrey changes my bandages while I try to ignore her, and the Italian cleaner in the black dress scrubs the floor and ignores me. Still, I don't need them. I get along fine myself.

"Grace, are you excited?" Audrey keeps talking to my back.

"Excited for what?" I ask the wall, wondering what's so exciting about staying alive. "Are you organizing a dance competition, and inviting me to participate?" What should I be excited about? That she's being forced to take care of me?

"Excited about going home." She brings the crutches closer and places them in front of my eyes, blocking my view of the wall.

"Who's going home?" I slowly get up and try not to look at her face, I don't want her to notice my surprise. Are they sending me home?

"You're going home," she answers as she hands me the crutches. "You have to get up and start getting ready."

"Am I on the list?" I struggle to stand by the side of the bed, holding the white metal frame for support and refusing to take the crutches from her. I'm not disabled. I never was.

"Yes, you're on the list. Your stay at Military Hospital 12 ends today. Soon they'll start reading the names of all the wounded who are going back home. Happily for you, you're on that list. The ship is already waiting at the port of Naples." She quickly replaces the sheet on my bed before I go back to lying in the position I've been in for the past two months. "From now on, you'll be taken care of in America."

"Are you sure?" It's probably a mistake. Does she think I've been cured?

"I'm sure you're going home," she replies as she places the rejected crutches by the wall. "You've received an exit ticket from the war back to our beloved nation. New York Harbor is waiting for you." She smiles at me. "I'll miss you, even though you were stubborn."

"But I'm not recovered yet." I look down.

"For you, the war is over." She smiles at me as I lie back in bed, turning my back to her again and staring at the old wall, searching for a new crack that's been wandering through the plaster for centuries.

"Grace, you'd better arrange your belongings. They'll be picking you up soon. You'll continue your recovery back home, along with the rest of the disabled." She puts her palm on my shoulder one last time, and I hear the sound of her shoes walking away down the hall. Now she's probably crossing the curtain separating my corner from the large hall where all the wounded men lie, going to tell someone else he's starting his journey home today.

"Grace, for you, the war is over," I whisper to the wall, looking down at where I once had a leg.

***

"Oliver," I hear one of the nurses after a while. She's standing in the center of the hall, among the other wounded soldiers. I scrape the old plaster from the wall with my fingertips, exposing more grooves within. I've been doing this for four months now, peeling the wall and examining it, looking for shapes within.

"Here," I hear Oliver answer.

"Stefan," she reads another name.

"Here."

Maybe Audrey was wrong. Maybe this is another list of the wounded, not those returning home.

I quickly get out of bed and sit down, standing and supporting myself as I grab the crutches leaning against the wall. I hate them, they hurt my armpits every time I try to use them to walk, as if reminding me that from now on I depend on them and the pain they bring. But I must know. Was Audrey wrong?

I carefully try to jump towards the window, leaning against its wooden frame and looking out at the wide parking lot in front of the hospital. She's not wrong.

A convoy of clean white ambulances stands on the road leading to the hospital, entering one by one and passing by the metal gate that was once the estate's barrier, and was now thrown to one side of the road. They slowly drive in and park at the entrance next to the large Red Cross flag spread on the ground, signaling to the sky and enemy aircraft that this complex is a hospital.

Maybe she was wrong after all? Maybe she won't call my name?

"Philip," the nurse continues to read off the list of names, and I turn around, looking at the great hall full of white metal beds and wounded soldiers.

"Going home." Philip sits down and answers while his friends greet him, wishing to be on the list next time. I stifle a scream of pain as a piece of wood gets lodged in my finger while I try to peel off the whitewashed window frame. She wasn't wrong.

"Owen," she continues, "going home." Some of his friends are clapping, and two approach and hug him.

"Malcolm." Another name on the list.

"I hope you can handle the German submarines," I hear someone laughing with him.

"If the Germans failed to kill me with their planes, nothing will kill me on my way home," he answers the one lying in bed next to him before getting up on his crutches, opening his metal locker, and packing his things. I can see Audrey approaching and helping him.

Soon the nurse will read my name. I should start packing my things, but how can I return home if I haven't recovered? Why are they sending me home for treatment with the other disabled wounded ones? I'm so young. I'm not disabled, I can't be disabled, I came here to save lives, I'm a nurse.

"George."

"We'll meet back home," he laughs, and I look at him shaking hands with his friends. I have to do something. I have to stay here, I'm too young to be in a wheelchair.

"Robert." She doesn't stop reading, walking through the great hall as she approaches me. I have to stay here. I have to go back to being who I was. I have to talk to someone to get me off the list, I'm only twenty-three years old.

"Grace," I hear my name.

What should I do?

"Grace."

I'll talk to someone. Surely there's someone who will listen to me.

"Grace!" she raises her voice and approaches me.

"Going home," I answer.

"Pack up your things. The ambulances are already waiting."

"I'm packing my things," I answer her, and hobble back with the crutches to my bed, looking at my belongings. They are tucked inside a small metal locker on the side of my bed. A hairbrush Audrey once gave me as a gift, some feminine things, and a small bag with my clothes. I'm not going to pack them, they're going to take me away from here. I'll talk to the head nurse on the second floor.

"Gilbert," the nurse holding the list walks away from me, back to the aisle between the men's beds. I have to hurry.

I hold the crutches again with both hands and start walking between the other wounded ones lying in the white beds in the hall. I'll talk to the head nurse, and she'll take me off the list. Click-clack, click-clack, I mustn't delay now. I lower my eyes as I walk down the passage between the straight rows of white beds.

"Grace, where are you going?"

"I forgot something. I'll be back in a second," I answer without turning my head, and try to walk out of this hall as fast as I can. I have to keep on walking, ignoring the pain in my armpits caused by the crutches that hate me.

"Did you pack your things?"

"Yes, they're already packed. I'll be back in a minute."

Why isn't she continuing to read the names from the list? She's probably watching me, she and all the other men in the hall, scrutinizing how I hobble while holding my crutches. It's not me. It's someone else. I have to climb the stairs to the second floor and reach the head nurse. I'll explain it to her, she'll understand.

***

"There's been a mistake," I tell her as soon as I enter her office at the end of the hall, coming through the door with the golden brass plaque attached: "Head Nurse".

"Sorry?" She raises her head and looks at me. She sits behind a large wooden desk covered in papers. Will she kick me out because I didn't knock and wait for her to call me inside?

"There's been a mistake on the list." I stand as steadily as I can in the center of her office, trying not to gasp from the effort of climbing the stairs. It took me a long time to climb the stairs, stopping several times to rest, trying not to think of my hurt leg.

"What kind of mistake?" She puts down the paper she's holding in her hands and looks at me, but even though I try to examine her, I can't tell if she's angry with me or will let me talk and explain. Her nurse's cap is tightly fastened to her black and silver striped hair.

"They're accidentally sending me back home."

"I don't think there's been a mistake here," she answers and goes back to reading, holding the paper at a distance. In a few years she'll need reading glasses. At least she isn't scolding me and kicking me out of her office.

"Please check your lists. An error has occurred here. They're sending me home." She must listen to me.

"I don't have to check my lists. I know your case. You're the only wounded female in my hospital. Your name is Grace. You recently came here from a hospital in Chicago where you started working as an intern nurse. You volunteered for the U.S. Medical Corps and joined a convoy from New York Harbor to Sicily, and from there you continued here to Italy. Four months ago you were injured in the major attack south of Rome. Fortunately for you, you survived the attack, and fortunately for you, your leg was amputated below the knee and not above it. And for you, the war is over," she says indifferently and goes back to reading the paper she's holding.

"Eight days," I whisper.

"What?" She doesn't raise her eyes from the paper.

"I just arrived," I want to shout at her that I had only been in Italy for eight days. "I need to recover. I can't stay like this."

"We gave you the best care we can here." She finally puts down the paper and looks at me. "They'll continue to treat your disability in America."

"But I still need to recover, to overcome my pain. I'm in pain," I say quietly. I hate that word she uses. I'm not like them.

"I'm sorry, but we can't arrange our schedule around your requests, we are at war, and it takes time for wounds to heal and for the pain to go away," she goes on, uttering the words from her red lipstick-painted lips.

"I need more time."

"Everyone needs more time, but we need your spot. There was another massive attack north of Florence. For some reason the Germans keep fighting, they don't want to surrender. There are a lot of new wounded on the way, and you know how it is. You also wanted to be a nurse once."

"Yes, I wanted to be a nurse too," I quietly answer, and I want to shout at her that I once was a nurse, not just wanting to be one. I was a nurse for eight whole days here in Italy, where I hardly slept and treated wounded soldiers coming from the front. And once I also smiled a nurse's perfect smile, with red lipstick matching my white uniforms, and it was just a few months ago that I boarded the ship at New York Harbor heading into the war in Europe.

"You'd better hurry. The convoy won't wait for you all day. The ship is already waiting at the port of Naples. They did us a favor sending us a ship to evacuate the wounded back home." She answers politely and goes back to reading the paper she's holding, hinting to me that the conversation between us is over.

"But there are German submarines at sea," I try, knowing it will no longer affect her. Nothing will change her decision, not even one injured woman who was once a nurse, or German submarines trying to sink any ship that crosses the Atlantic.

"Don't you think you should trust the Lord, who is watching over you?" She looks up from the paper again, and I lower my gaze, examining my bare foot. Once I had two, but now instead of my feet there is only a blank piece of ugly white hospital pant leg. Even though God kept me alive, my leg is gone. Maybe he shouldn't have tried so hard.

"Thank you, head nurse," I answer and turn to leave.

"Blanche, my name is Blanche," she answers as she begins writing something on the paper. "And please close the door behind you."

"Yes, head nurse Blanche," I whisper, and lean on my crutches, releasing my hand and closing the door. I have to hurry, the convoy is leaving soon. I must do something.

***

"Where did Grace go?" I hear the voice of the nurse, the one reading the notes. I lean against the wall near the on-call nurse's door, trying to catch my breath. I'm not used to walking so much with the crutches. In a moment they'll start looking for me.

How can I go home like this, a lame rag doll on crutches that everyone is staring at with pity? Wheelchairs are for older people who can't walk anymore, not for young women like me.

"She went up into the hallway," I hear someone answer. What should I do?

I'm not disabled. I must get out of this convoy.

"She said she'll right back." The nurse from the hall is talking to someone else, maybe Audrey, the nurse who likes me. Will she help me escape?

"I'll help you look for her." It seems that it's her, and after a moment, as I peek from the hallway towards the stairs, I see her climbing towards me.

"Grace, you have to pack, the convoy is leaving soon. I'll help you down the stairs."

"I can't go with the convoy. They'll make me disabled in a wheelchair at home." I start to cry.

"I'm so sorry," she approaches and hugs me. "But there's nothing we can do, you have to go."

"Please help me stay." I hug her. "Please, just some more time." She's the only one here who cares for me.

"I'm sorry, I can't, you'll be fine back home. They have a special place where they'll teach you everything you need to know."

"But I'm twenty-three," I whisper to her in tears.

"Come down with me. I'll help you pack." She stops hugging me.

"I'll be right there," I whisper to her. "I'll just wash my face and I'll come."

"Shall I help you down the stairs?"

"No, it's okay," I wipe my eyes. "Can you start packing my things?"

She gives me a little hug and goes down the stairs, disappearing into the main hall. I have to hurry, they're going to take me. I can't go home and be crippled.

I hold the crutches firmly and try to walk down the stairs leading to the entrance, but I stop and look down. After my injury, I've never gone down stairs. How will I go down without falling?

I reach out and try to hold the railing with my hand, supporting my body with my hand and jumping down the first step. But the crutches loosen and fall noisily down the stairs to the bottom. I've lost my support. Did they hear the noise in the hall? Will they come looking for me?

"I'll try jumping one step," I whisper to myself, gripping the railing tightly, jumping down and almost falling.

"And one more," I whisper and grab the railing, hoping Audrey won't come looking for me again.

"And one more." I'm panting.

"Help me," I beg the Italian cleaner in the black dress who's starting to go up the stairs.

She stops and looks at the crutches lying at her feet on the floor, then looks up at me.

"Please," I whisper to her. In all those months she cleaned my corner every morning, I never spoke to her. Maybe in the beginning, when I was in so much pain and yelling, not remembering who I spoke to. But I don't think she understands me now.

She starts going up the stairs and looks at me with her dark eyes. She doesn't understand. But when she gets close to me, and I think she's going to pass me by, she takes my hand and wraps it around her shoulder, holds my hand tightly, and hugs my body with her other hand, supporting me as we slowly go down together, me leaning against her body, trying not to gasp at the jumps down the stairs.

Would she be helping me if she knew I was running away?

"Thanks," I smile at her when we reach the first floor, and she helps me lean against the wall. She bends over, collects the crutches lying on the floor, and hands them to me, not saying anything. She just turns her back and goes up the stairs, ignoring me.

"Thank you," I whisper to her again, and hurry as much as I can, passing the building's large front door and ignoring the pain that's started in the amputated leg. I have to hurry. If I can just manage to go to the hospital's garden without them noticing, they won't find me there, and the convoy will go without me.

The white ambulances are parking in front of the hospital entrance with their back doors already open, ready to welcome the wounded, and all the drivers are gathered around one of them, talking to each other and enjoying the warm morning sun. Will they notice me? I have to act like I'm a regular injured person, it's a hospital, there's a lot of wounded people here.

I slowly hobble towards the back of the building as I lean on the crutches, careful not to slip and fall. I mustn't rush, I'm not used to them, I never agreed to go out to the garden before.

"Let's go outside, the garden is in front of the sea, the warm air will make you feel good," Audrey used to tell me every morning, smiling at me with her big eyes and red lipstick. But I refused, and insisted on lying in bed in front of the wall, looking at the plaster lifelines of the cracks in the wall. Now I have to cross the parking lot, they want to take me away from my wall.

Just a few more steps, I count the line of clean white ambulances, they're not like the ones we had at the front, which were khaki and filthy with mud. Just a few more steps to the end of the parking lot, I can make it.

"Excuse me, are you with us?" One of the drivers is approaching. He probably wants to help me. I don't need help.

"No, I'm with the next convoy." I continue to walk, trying to keep smiling even when my bare feet step on the sharp stones, does he notice that I don't wear shoes?

"Good luck. Do you need help?"

"No thanks, I'm fine." I keep walking, hoping he won't try to be a gentleman and escort me, and to my relief he returns to his friends who are gathered around a wooden box with the medical corps emblem on it. Some of them bend over and hold cards, place coins and gamble, while the rest stand around and watch them, attaching money to the game. Just a few more steps up to the path that leads to the garden.

The garden behind the hospital is empty in the early morning hours, and the white deckchairs on the grass are empty by now, arranged in straight lines ending at the cliff facing the sea, waiting for the wounded. Later they'll stroll through the garden, supported by the nurses, or just sit motionless in the wide chairs and look to the horizon, waiting for evening, for the nurses to pick them up and take them back to their beds. To this day I sometimes stand at the window, looking at them in the garden, refusing to go out. I'm not as they are.

The grass feels soft to my bare foot, but I must not stop here and sit, not even to rest, they must be looking for me already. I keep crossing the green path, careful not to slip on the grass still wet with the morning dew. I have to keep moving forward, find a place to hide. I direct my steps to an old stone shed at the end of the garden. A few more steps and I'll be safe.

Just behind the old shed wall, I allow myself to stop and rest for a moment. Even though it's early in the morning, I'm all sweating; my bare foot is bleeding from the sharp stones that injured me as I crossed the hospital parking lot. I should have put my shoe on, but then the nurse with the list of names would suspect me. What will I do now?

I carefully lean against the shed wall and sit down, feeling the rough stone wall scratch my back through the hospital pajamas. I'll stay here. They won't find me here. The ambulances will go on without me.

"Grace!" I hear the nurses calling in the garden. Did the ambulance driver tell them he saw me? Will they come pick me up? I cling to the wall and try not to move or make noise, but I know it doesn't matter. If they just get behind the shed, they'll find me. Maybe I should give up and go home, what does it even matter? How long will I be able to run from the convoy?

I try to crawl and hold the crutches, but it's too hard. I have to rest, just a few more minutes, but the voices calling my name are coming closer.

I take a few breaths, crawl to the crutches again, hold them, get up and keep on moving, stepping towards the stone wall surrounding the mansion and the grove of cypresses and olive trees behind it. I must reach the grove, it's the only place I can hide from the voices crying out my name. My bare foot is scratched by sharp stones as I climb the wall, but I have to cross it and get out of the garden. I hold onto the stones with all my might. I have to succeed, I have no other choice, I've already thrown the crutches over the stone fence, I have no way back.

The engine noise from approaching planes makes me cringe, and I feel exposed while holding myself to the stone fence, unable to escape or even bend without falling. All I can do is lower my gaze and close my eyes and wait for the machinegun noise to hit me while I try to shrink and become part of the stones, as the sounds of aircraft engines get louder. But the noise passes over me, and when I finally open my eyes and look at the sky, I see the large green bodies of two bombers with the blue circle and white star of the U.S. Air Force painted on their wings. These are not German planes. Slowly they drop and disappear behind the treetops, approaching the military airfield behind the hill.

"Grace!" I hear the shouts in the garden again. I must cross the wall. I manage to pull myself over the stone wall and fall on the other side, trying to support myself as much as I can. Still, my amputated stump hits the ground, and even though I try to stifle my scream, I fail, and scream in pain, looking at my pants and seeing a red stain spread on the white cloth, dirty from the ground. I've opened the wound that had healed.

Get up, ignore the pain, keep walking, do not look at your pants. I have to get away.

I keep walking in the woods, supported by my crutches, looking for a place to hide. Please don't hear me. Between a row of bushes, I lie on the hard ground and tuck the sleeve of my shirt into my mouth, biting it with my teeth, holding my shouts back. I don't care about the tears of pain flowing down my cheeks. Please don't hear my cries. Please don't take me from here and make me crippled.

***

Hours later, after I see the ambulance convoy leaving the

hospital and heading south on the road to Naples, only then do I get up from my hiding place in the bushes and try to stand upright. My whole body hurts, and I walk slowly, looking for a passage through the stone fence through which I can return to the hospital. I can't jump over the wall again, I'm too afraid to stumble and hit my stump on the ground. My leg is full of scratches and blood, and my arms are scratched from my fingernails. I've hurt myself, doing anything to keep quiet when I heard them searching for me.

It takes me a while to find a spot where the stone fence is ruined, with a big hole in it. It's probably a remnant of the war fought here and passed on north, a tank shell or a bomb from a plane, and I slowly step through the gaping opening in the wall, careful not to slip on the sharp stones. I hobble to the old shed, leaning against its wall that hides me from the hospital. I have to rest again, I'll try to be as quiet as I can. When the day is over, and the injured men in the garden go inside, I'll try to sneak in with them. I have no idea what I'll say to the nurses, but I'll think of something, they'll understand. I was like them too, once.

"What about the amputee nurse? Did they find her? I think she managed to escape." I hear two nurses talking to each other across the wall, and smell their cigarette smoke. They must be close to me.

"She didn't get on the convoy. She shouldn't have joined the war at all," the second one answers her.

"She wasn't even really a nurse, just an intern." That sounds like Audrey.

"They shouldn't have sent her to the front."

"I don't know why they sent an unprofessional person like her to the front lines. She's just arrived and now she's returning home."

"At least she wants to stay."

"She needs to know her place. She's disabled. She needs to be taken care of. She can't become a nurse again." I hear Audrey and cringe.

"Who would want her like that at home?" the other nurse answers Audrey. "Luckily I'm not in her place."

"Yeah, no one would want her at home. Too bad for her. I feel sorry for her. She could be so beautiful if she hadn't lost her leg." My fingers tightly grip the sleeve of my shirt.

"She just didn't realize she had to stay away from German pilots," one of them laughs.

"Yes, better to choose our pilots." The other one also starts laughing.

"Where were you? We're looking for you," I hear another voice. "New casualties from the front just arrived, we need your help." Their speech fades away with bursts of laughter.

My fingers slowly crumble the reddish terracotta plaster off the old wall. I'll stay here a little longer, I'm comfortable here when I lean against the shed wall. I can handle my pain here.

***

The cool night breeze blows in my face as I finally rise and walk toward the dark hospital building, passing the garden between the empty lounge chairs. I have to drink and eat something, I didn't eat anything all day, and the pain in my amputated leg has intensified from prolonged sitting. I need some help from the nurses.

In the silence that surrounds me, I can hear the sound of the waves in the distance. My hands ache from holding the crutches all day, but I ignore the pain and approach the old mansion-turned-hospital. In the dark all around, only a few windows in the building shed light into the night, like eyes staring at me accusingly. Still I ignore them, I must go inside, I must find Audrey, maybe she'll agree to take care of me, even though I don't know my place and shouldn't be here, and I'm no longer beautiful without my leg. I have no one else to ask for help. After that, I'll return to my corner and wait quietly until the next ship takes me home. I promise myself that I won't shout, even if I'm in pain.

The parking lot at the hospital entrance is empty of ambulances, and only a few military vehicles are parked on the side next to each other like a black mass. In the distance I notice two large cypresses at the entrance near the ruined gate. Step by step I pass the vehicles in the parking lot, past the large canvas of the Red Cross flag spread out in the center of the parking lot. It looks almost black in the faint light of the moon, but

I ignore it and look towards the entrance to the mansion, praying no one will see me at such a late hour and that everyone is asleep except the nurse on call.

I have to sit and use my hands to go up the entrance stairs, climbing them one by one, dragging the crutches behind me and trying not to make noise. I have no more strength to stand and jump, but it doesn't seem to bother anyone. The great hall is dark, and only a faint light emanates from the nurses' station, where one of them sits and listens to the radio quietly playing jazz music. But it's not Audrey. A few more steps, and I'll get to my corner.

Even the wounded are quiet in the dark room, and no one tells me anything as I walk between the rows of straight beds towards mine, occasionally stopping to breathe and rest while looking at the floor with downcast eyes, careful not to stumble in the dark. With a few more steps, I'll reach my corner, and I can lie down and go to sleep, I'll give up on food.

But when I get to my corner and feel the metal frame of the bed, I quickly pull my hand back. My bed is no longer mine.

They gave my bed to someone else, they've left me no place to be. Another soldier is lying there. Even the small locker that was once mine stands next to the bed that is already his.

What was I thinking? That they would save my place for me? Those nurses who thought it was a pity I didn't go, that I don't belong here? Why didn't I go with the convoy? How will I stay here now?

As I hold onto the bed frame so as not to fall, I approach the wounded man and examine him in the dark, but I can hardly see his face, only the bandages covering his head and eyes. I can't even hear his breathing, even when I bring my head closer to him. Is he still alive? Shall I call the shift nurse?

I gently touch his lips with the tip of my finger. They are hot. He is alive.

I'll wait here until morning, by my bed. I'll take care of him, see that he's alive. I sit on the floor at the foot of his bed, holding myself from drinking the glass of water next to his bed. Putting my back to the wall, I try to ignore the pain in my leg, but it gets harder, same as it was after they removed my leg, and I scratch the wall and my thighs, trying not to cry.

"Soon the morning will arrive," I whisper to the wall. "Soon they'll give me something for the pain. Wall, do you hear? Does it hurt you when I peel pieces of plaster from you?"

***

3. Unwanted.

"Good morning, Gracie, how do you feel this morning after everyone was looking for you yesterday?" I open my eyes and see Audrey smiling. She leans over me as I sit on the floor under my occupied bed, my back against the wall while I raise my eyes to her. Her smooth brown hair is neat and collected, and she smells of soap. I touch my head, feeling my messy hair.

"Are you thirsty?" she asks, and I just nod my head while she strokes my arm. Then she gets up and walks away, coming back after a moment and serving me a glass of milk and a bowl of porridge.

"Thanks," I hoarsely whisper to her

as I sip from the bowl, continuing to watch her as she rises and stands over me, checking the sleeping wounded man in my bed. She has a beautiful body with an ample chest, and I lower my gaze and examine her clean white nurse's dress and her two legs standing safely on the floor by the stranger's bed. She's not as ugly as I am.

"Grace."

"Yes," I look up at her.

"The head nurse wants to talk to you." She smiles at me with her red lipstick.

"Yes," I answer as I chew the porridge.

"Now, she wants to see you now." She takes the bowl from my hands, even though I haven't finished yet.

I wipe my mouth with my palm and comb my hair with my fingers, trying to fix it. I also try to wipe the soil residue and bloodstains from my dirty pajamas, a reminder of yesterday's scratches. I need to be tidy, the head nurse wants to see me.

Click-clack, click-clack. I cross the hall and look down, knowing that all the previous wounded ones are watching me now, the amputee who escaped from the convoy yesterday. They're explaining who I am to the new ones. I should ignore them, I'll explain everything to the head nurse.

It takes time for me to go up to the second floor, it also takes time for me to stand by the closed door to her room and catch my breath. It also takes time for me to knock on the door and wait for her to call me inside.

"What am I going to do with you now? I have a whole hospital to manage, and one wounded woman who thinks she's above military rules and deserves special treatment," head nurse Blanche talks to me, but I don't look at her. I'm standing tall and looking ahead to the window behind her, from which I can see the blue sea spreading from her window to the horizon. The crutches hurt me when I lean on them, but I keep standing still.

I was wrong. I was so wrong. No one will take care of me anymore, she doesn't need someone like me here either.

"I have nowhere to put you. I don't need you here." She keeps talking, and I look for a moment at the white nurse's hat attached to her silver hair, and her bright eyes staring at me, lifting my chin back and looking at the blue sea again. No one here will help me recover.

"What will I do with you?" she asks me again, but she does not seem to intend that I answer her. I have nowhere to go, I have no bed to sleep in either, what can I say to her?

"I can help in the hospital in the meantime. I'm a nurse," I whisper. Or I used to be one once, at least.

"Help me in the hospital? Doing what?"

"I'm a nurse." I try to stand as tall as I can.

"You mean an inexperienced intern nurse."

"I'm a nurse," I repeat, wanting to tell her how many wounded soldiers I treated in those few days before I was injured. At some point, I stopped counting.

"What kind of intern were you? An OR nurse?" She looks at me, checking my dirty pajamas.

"Yes, Head Nurse Blanche."

"And can you treat my wounded in the operation room, with your leg?"

"No, Head Nurse Blanche." I keep standing straight but I know it won't help me.

"So you're no longer a nurse, you're a cripple who should have been sitting on the deck of a U.S. Army hospital ship, on your way to New York Harbor, drinking hot American Army milk and being excited to see the Statue of Liberty appear on the horizon."

"Yes, Head Nurse Blanche,"

"And now you're holding up a bed I need for a wounded soldier, I have no extra bed to give you." She keeps looking at me, as if reading from a list of accusations.

"Yes, Head Nurse Blanche." I don't answer that someone else has already taken my bed.

"Go to the nurses and ask them to try to arrange a place for you to sleep."

"Yes, Head Nurse Blanche." I make sure to stand straight, even though it's hard for me to lean that way. I won't show her that it's difficult for me, even though she doesn't care.

"And return to your corner, you're going home with the next convoy."

"Yes, Head Nurse Blanche." I don't want to tell her that I have no corner anymore either.

"And find someone to take care of your leg. You were injured. You must be treated."

"Yes, Head Nurse Blanche."

"And get out of my office."

"Yes, Head Nurse Blanche."

"And call me Blanche."

"Yes, Head Nurse Blanche." I take

one last look at the sea inviting me to come visit, so blue in the summer morning sun. Then I turn around and hobble away, leaving her office.

***

"Audrey, I apologize, Blanche asked that you help me find a place to sleep." I enter the nurse's station, which is just a small room in the corner of the hall. Maybe it used to be the servants' waiting room before the war, when they used to have balls or receptions at the mansion. Now it's been converted into the on-call nurse's room, full of pills and medicine shelves, syringes and morphine vials.

"Gracie, you should call her Head

Nurse Blanche," Audrey answers as she continues to read the book she's holding, sitting behind a small wooden table in the center of the room.

"Sorry, Head Nurse Blanche asked that you help me find a bed." I stand up straight and look around, examining the shelves laden with pill bottles in all varieties of color, as if from a sweet candy store.

"One moment," she raises her head from the book for the first time and looks at me. "In the meantime, please wait outside," she smiles at me. "The entrance to this room is only for nurses."

"Yes, Nurse Audrey." I step outside the small room and stand at the entrance, watching her eyes pass over the pages while she mumbles the words to herself until she reaches the end of the chapter, moves the bookmark to its new place, closes the book, stands up and smiles at me.

"Let's find you a place to sleep." She passes me, walking down the aisle between the beds. "We don't want you to sleep outside in the garden like you tried to do yesterday."

The main hall is full of the newly-wounded, to the point that the beds almost touch each other, barely allowing the nurses room to move and take care of them. All the wounded men sent home yesterday have been replaced by new ones, as if they had never been here at all.

"The Third Division failed to break the German lines," Audrey turns around and tells me as she stops for a moment next to one of the new ones, helping him sit up in bed. "A lot of wounded arrived yesterday." She keeps walking as she talks to me: "You should have gone home, even if you think you're in pain and that you need more time to recover. We must obey regulations." She smiles at another new one, stroking his black hair gently. "Isn't that what you were taught in the nurses' course?"

"Yes, obeying regulations is what we were taught in the nurses' course," I answer and feel the pain in my leg, remembering the woman who recruited me back in Chicago.

"You're volunteering for the war," the recruiting nurse told us then, in Chicago. She was standing on stage in a hall full of excited nurses like me. Above our heads hung a sign spread from side to side, calling for war volunteers. "You will be sent overseas," she continued to speak as she raised her voice. It was unnecessary, we were all fascinated by the war and willing to contribute to our nation. "You will take care of the war wounded in Europe and the Pacific. You will see blood." She paused for a moment and looked around with her red lips, reviewing all the nurses who had come to the conference. "The main thing you should take with you to the war from Chicago is your professionalism." She paused for a moment, "This is not a game, this is war. You'll be in the army, and the army works according to rules. You must be more professional than you are here in Chicago. You can't feel pity for combat soldiers. The wounded mustn't think that you feel sorry for them, or sad about what's happened to them. You must be professional. They, like you, volunteered to serve our nation. They are proud, like you are now." She finished and came down from the stage to shake our hands, and we all got up from our chairs and hurried to the registration booth.

"We'll have to re-register you. I deleted you from our lists yesterday." She continues walking down the aisle, searching for a bed.

"Thanks," I whisper, wanting to shout that she shouldn't have erased me, that I just want to recover here like any of the other wounded around us, the ones she's so kind towards. I'm not to blame for the Germans fighting so hard. They cut my leg off too, I didn't do it to myself.

"Grace, you'll have to share your corner with the wounded man who's already there. The main hall is full," she tells me when she finally comes back. She pushes a white bed, carefully maneuvering it down the aisle, and placing it by the bed of the wounded soldier who took my bed last night.

Now, in the daylight, I can finally see him. He is lying in bed like all the others, but unlike them, his eyes are also covered with white bandages wrapped around his head. Only his lips and unshaven chin are visible, and his black hair sticking through the bandages.

What will I do? How will I be next to him? Our beds are so close to each other, only the small metal locker that was once mine separates us. I have never slept so close to a man, feeling his presence, even if he's injured and his eyes are covered with bandages.

"What about intimacy?" I ask Audrey. Before today, I'd had a curtain to hide me from other eyes, my private corner that protected me from all the other men in the hall. How would I clean up next to him? And what about the rest?

"I'm sorry, you really should have gone back home with the ship and not stayed here." She pushes the wounded man's bed even further, placing him by the wall that was mine, the one I always used to talk to and scratch at night.

"You'll have to get along with him. It doesn't really matter to him," she continues to talk as she spreads clean sheets on my new bed. "He can't see, his eyes were injured, and even if he lives he'll remain blind." She turns to him and gently strokes his black hair before talking to me again. "Let me help you clean up."

"It's okay. I'll clean up on my own."

"Are you sure?"

"Yes, thank you, Nurse Audrey."

"As you wish." She places bandages and iodine on the small metal locker, and again strokes the hair of the quiet wounded man now lying next to me. "I'll come by soon to see how he is doing." She turns her back to me and walks away,

drawing the curtain separating
us from the rest of the wounded
soldiers in the hall.

I look at him again, examining his chest that peacefully rises and falls under the white sheet, looking at his eyes covered with thick bandages. Everything is fine, he can't see me, he's badly injured and fighting for his life.

I sit on my new bed and turn my back on him, opening button after button as I take off my pajama shirt and slowly clean my body with the sponge, shivering for a moment at the touch of the cold water.

"He can't see me," I whisper to myself as I roll down my hospital pants. I won't look in his direction.

He's not here, it's just me and my wall that already knows my body. My hand gently rubs my thighs as I clean myself, keeping my back to him.

After that, I keep quiet when I put iodine on my wound and cover my amputated leg with new bandages, feeling no pity for myself like a proud nurse. But the tears keep flowing down my cheeks, and I can hear my heavy breathing as I hold myself back from screaming in pain, so glad he's unconscious and can't hear my sighs.

"Did you manage?" Audrey asks me later when she pulls back the curtain and comes to check on him.

"Yes, thank you." I lie in bed,

waiting for the pain to go away,
scratching my hips.

"Next time," she smiles at me,
"try to stay here and not run away
when the ship arrives. You just
injured yourself again. You have to
remember that even though you're
not a nurse anymore, obeying
the rules is always good for the
wounded as well."

***

I'm in pain. The hospital is quiet late
at night, except for the soft music
coming from the nurses' room. I
can't fall asleep while I lie all sweaty
in my bed, trying to overcome
the pain in my leg that has come
back. I scratch my hips with my

fingernails, sighing and trying not to cry for help.

I have to get something to help with the pain, a shot of morphine, just one shot to let me fall asleep like earlier, when the nurses had agreed to help me.

I try to get up, sending my hand towards the wall, but the silent wounded man's bed prevents me from reaching it. I can't even peel the plaster from the wall, and my fingers scratch my arms as hard as I can while I bite my lips, but the pain in my amputated leg continues.

"Please stop, please stop," I whisper to the pain. I can't go on like this, and I feel the tears in my eyes when another wave of pain comes.

"Please, leave!" I bite the white

sheet spread on the bed, trying not to whine, but when the next wave of pain washes over me, I can't hold myself back from sighing, pushing my face into the mattress. Maybe it's good that there's music in the hall, so no one hears me.

What should I do? I scratch my leg, trying to hurt myself elsewhere, anything to stop those pangs, but it doesn't help. I can't hold myself back anymore, I have to ask for something to soothe the pain. My whole leg burns with agony caused by the scratches I've made with my nails.

"Audrey, I'm in pain. I need morphine." I stand in front of the little nurses' room, tightly gripping my crutches.

"Gracie, I'm sorry, I can't give you any." She looks up from her book.

"I need it. It hurts so much."

"Gracie, you know you were addicted to it."

"But I'm in pain, just one shot, I'm not addicted," I search for the narcotics shelf in her little room. "I'm strong enough to handle it." My hands grip the crutches tightly.

"No, you're not." She closes her book. "I've seen strong soldiers get injured, you're not one of them."

"I am. I'm a nurse like you, I've treated injured soldiers like you. I've seen things."

"Gracie, how long have you been an intern nurse?" She gets up from her chair and approaches me.

"A long time, ever since I landed in Italy and until I was injured," I answer her, not wanting her to know it had only been eight days.

"Italy wasn't a long time ago, although to you it may seem like an eternity." She looks at me. "A few days isn't a long time. Two years is a long time. I was in the first wave that landed in North Africa in 1942, when it all started." She looks down at my missing leg, and I lower my eyes, wanting to turn around and hobble back to my place. "Aspirin, that's the most you'll get from me," she keeps talking, and I reach my hand out to her like a beggar. I don't like it when she calls me Gracie. "I'm glad you understand." She smiles and turns her back to me, taking a handful of pills from one of the glass jars on the shelves and pouring them into a small jar for me.

"Thank you," I whisper to her, holding the pills tightly. "They'll help me." But I know that by nighttime they won't be enough.

"Gracie," she calls me as I turn around and start walking by to my corner.

"Yes?" I turn back to her.

"Gracie, Do you smoke?"

"No." I want to tell her my name is Grace.

"Start smoking," She walks over to me, taking a box of cigarettes out of her white uniform and stuffing it in my pajama pocket. "If you haven't seen enough injured soldiers to start smoking, then maybe you should look at yourself and realize that it's time for you to start. Who knows, maybe it'll calm you down."

"Thanks."

"You're welcome, and if you're bored, you can always read a book." She goes back for a moment, takes the book lying on the table and gives it to me. "We nurses have too much work anyway, we don't have free time to read. Now get back to your bed and get some rest, I can see you're sweating."

"Thanks," I answer quietly, but she's already turned her back and headed to talk to one of the other nurses who's entered the hall.

"Are you coming to the pilots' club tomorrow?" I hear the other nurse ask Audrey as I slowly hobble away, supported by my crutches, careful not to drop the book and the jar of pills.

"Sure I'm coming, are you coming too?" Audrey answers. "I like one of them, and I need a break from all the work here."

"I hope it's not the handsome one that I like," the other nurse laughs, and they lean into each other and whisper.

"Pick me up in the evening. I'll be ready." I can still hear Audrey answering her when the other nurse leaves the hall.

"I'll be ready tonight too," I whisper to myself as I walk to my bed. I have a book and aspirin pills to fight the pain.

My fingers fumble for the aspirin jar on the metal locker, and I open it, pour its contents out and swallow some pills, feeling them burn in my throat. I don't care that I don't have any water, I won't touch the glass of water that belongs to the quiet wounded man, not even one small sip.

How much time has passed? I feel the sweat on my back, I should count the minutes until the pills start working. "Please, pain, stop," I whisper. I have a book, I can read the book.

My shaking hands hold the book she left me. I'll try to read it. "Wall, do you hear? I will read to you." Maybe even the silent wounded man will listen. I need light.

I have a candle in the drawer, but I don't have matches or a lighter. Maybe the silent man has one?

"Do you have a lighter?" I ask him, knowing he won't answer. Would it bother him if I looked for a lighter in his bag? I don't think it would bother him at all, he's almost dead anyway.

"I apologize, I have to," I whisper to him as my hand searches for his bag, which has been thrown inside the locker. I feel the remnants of mud covering the bag peel off and fall to the floor. "I'm only looking through the bag's pocket. I just need your lighter for a moment, my leg hurts so much."

"Thanks," I say to him as I feel the cold metal touch of the lighter, and I pull it out and light the candle, place it on the locker, lean back and open the book.

"Do you want me to read to you?" I ask him, and start reading without waiting for an answer. If I stop for just a moment, I won't be able to continue. I must try not to think about the wave of pain that has coursed through my leg, as though it were waiting for the dark night. I must keep reading, mumbling the words and thinking of something else. "Do you hear?" I ask the wounded man after a while. "The heroine has a beautiful dress, and now she's on her way to prom, but all that interests her now is that she's really in pain, but the author didn't dare write that in the book, he thought they'd think she isn't a heroine. What do you think about dances? Are you even alive, or as still as the wall? But the wounded man doesn't answer me. Maybe he isn't alive? Every now and then I put my fingertip to his lips, feeling their heat or wetting them with some water, just to avoid thinking about the pain.

"Nurse Audrey, do you hear?" I whisper when a new wave of pain strikes my leg, and my fingers crumple the pages, gripping them tightly. "I've overcome the pain, I'm reading your book." I wipe the tears with my fingers, trying to straighten the wet and crumpled pages. Soon the pain will pass.

But the morning refuses to come, and I read page after page to the wounded man, I mustn't stop.

"Head Nurse Blanche, do you hear?" I stifle a shout as I scratch the book cover during the next wave of pain. "I am a nurse, I'm taking care of someone, I've read him a story." But I can no longer hold on anymore, and I grab the book and toss it against the wall, bending over the bed and filling my mouth with the white sheet, suffocating my sobs.

"Here, you can see, I'm a trained nurse. I can treat another wounded person," I keep whispering to the silent man as I wipe my tears away.

"I've even managed to wet your lips with some water, or maybe those are my tears, but you don't mind," I whisper to him as I stroke his lips with my wet fingers.

Breathe slowly, let the wave of pain pass, get out of bed, and look for the book on the floor. I'll read to him a little longer, maybe the wounded man is in pain too.

"Help me," I say to the silent Italian cleaner when she approaches me, "please, help me."

She turns to me and says nothing. "Please, I need you to help me," I whisper to her as she approaches, and I look at her, trying to see her face in the dim light. Does she understand what I'm saying? "I need you to help me move something," I whisper to her again, not wanting the nurses to hear over the music coming from their room. Even though I'm not sure she understands me, she comes closer while I get out of my bed again and stand by the silent wounded man. "I need you to help me change our beds," I say to her. "I need to be by the wall." I lean my crutches against the peeling wall and support myself with the metal bed frame, starting to pull and move it. "It doesn't matter to him," I explain to her as we move the beds. "He's blind and silent, he doesn't see anything anyway."

But she says nothing. She just finishes moving the beds with me and hands me the crutches, ignoring my sweaty face and sighs. Maybe she didn't notice, maybe she just didn't understand.

"Thanks," I whisper to her as she walks away and resumes cleaning. I follow her with my eyes as she bends over between the beds of the wounded men in the dark, disappearing with her black dress, leaving me alone with my pain and the silent wounded man.

"Sorry," I explain to him, sighing as my fingers crumble the plaster. "I needed my wall. It doesn't matter to you anyway." But he doesn't answer me.

"It hurts so much," I wipe tears of pain from my cheeks, reaching my hand out and tightly gripping his bed's metal frame. "Are you in pain, even though you're silent?" In the dark, I can't tell if he's breathing at all. "Are you alive?" I ask, not expecting an answer, but I manage to get a little closer, reaching my hand out and feeling his lips. They're still warm. "You're alive. They must have given you morphine so you wouldn't suffer, and now you're in a dreamland." My fingers wet his lips with some water from the glass next to his bed. "Don't get used to it. When they quiet you down, the pain will make you want to die."

***

"I'm glad you took my advice," I hear Nurse Audrey's voice the following morning, and turn my eyes from the wall. She stands by the silent man's bed and looks at the open book thrown onto our shared locker.

"That really helped." I sit up in bed and hold the book, not wanting her to notice its crumpled pages. I also take back the crushed cigarette box thrown onto the locker, trying to straighten it after clutching it last night.

"I'm glad it hurts less. What happened to the beds?" She begins to change the silent wounded man's bandages.

"Last night I had almost no pain at all. The Italian cleaner moved them," I gently caress my scratched knees, careful not to accidentally touch the amputation below. I'll have to ask her for iodine for the scratches.

"You know," she continues talking to me, "I also wanted to be deployed to the front as a nurse. But I decided I wanted to be by their side when they wake up in the hospital, to be the one helping them recover." She bends down and gets close to him, her white dress and chest almost touching his body. "John, how are you this morning?" Her fingers stroke his hair.

"I wanted to save lives," I whisper to the crumpled box of cigarettes I hold in my hand. "I wanted to be the one who kept them alive until they got here." I tuck the cigarettes deep inside my shirt pocket and look at Audrey. She sprinkles sulfa disinfectant powder on his chest, making sure not to soil her white uniform with the powder.

"Don't you think those are decisions we should leave to God?" She smiles at me and turns back to him. "John, how are your wounds today?" She takes his open pajamas to the sides. "Gracie wants to take the Lord's role on the battlefield, she wants to be the one to decide whether you should live or die. But it seems to me we should leave that decision to the true God, don't you think?"

"That's not what I meant," I answer, wanting to crumple the pages of the book I'm holding again.

"I know," she smiles at me. "I was just kidding, but it doesn't matter to John anyway, does it, John?"She looks at the bandages she's replaced for him with satisfaction. "Now let's see how you are. It'd be best if you didn't go running around again. Does the amputation hurt now?" She smiles at me.

"It doesn't hurt at all." I grab the sheet tightly and smile at her. "Can I replace the bandages myself? I want to practice."

"Are you sure you can?" She looks at me.

"Yes, I have to study."

"Less work for me." She places the jar of sulfa powder and bandages on the white locker. "If you fail it, call me." She strokes John's hair again.

"Bye, John, and make sure to rest." She turns her back and walks away to the hall where all the wounded are.

"How long should I rest?"

"About a month, until the next ship arrives."

***

"John?" I get closer to him after she leaves. "John, can you hear me? I'm Grace, the one who was in pain last night." I examine his lips and the bandages over his eyes. "Nice to meet you." I extend my hand and touch his fingers, shaking his hand.

His fingertips are warm, but he doesn't respond to my touch, and I can only notice his chest rising and falling with every breath he takes.

"John, did you hear Audrey?" I speak to him a little later. "If you live, you have a month to be by my side while I rest, a month to hear my sighs at night." But he does not respond.

"I wanted to be a nurse and take care of the wounded," I whisper to him, even though we're both alone in the corner of the hall, separated from the others, and I don't have to whisper. "But I probably won't tell anyone I'm a nurse anymore, I'll just rest and wait here for the pain to come at night, until they send me home."

***

"Give me something to do." I stand next to Audrey, who is changing a bandage for a wounded soldier in the hall.

"Gracie, you should return to bed, your job is to rest." She pauses for a moment and turns to me.

"Give me something to do. Let me help you." I try to stay stable as I lean on my crutches.

"You can't help me. You're injured. You need to lie down and rest."

"I'm a nurse like you."

"Gracie, you're no longer a nurse like us, you never were, even if you really wanted to be," she says, before returning to hold the wounded man's hand.

"But you have a shortage of nurses,

don't you?" I hand her the scissors, trying not to lose my balance, careful not to slip in front of the other wounded men watching us now.

"Thank you." She takes them. "We're at war, we always have a shortage of nurses, but we know how to manage with the ones we have." She begins to cut his bandage, exposing the wound.

"So let me help you." I hand her the bandages. "I don't want to lie down all day. I'll do whatever you need."

"Is there something wrong with your corner? John's company shouldn't bother you. He's blind and barely alive." She looks at me again for a moment. "Or does it bother you, and you want your privacy? Do you know we're at war?" She hands the scissors back and puts iodine on his wound.

"No, he's not bothering me at all, and yes, we're at war, and I came to the war as an intern nurse. I want to learn."

"You came to this place to rest and wait for the ship back home, not to be an intern nurse. We don't need you to help us here. We get along." She looks at me for another moment. "Maybe the Italian cleaner who usually curses everyone is looking for help." She smiles at me before turning her back and moving on to the next wounded soldier, asking him how he's feeling, leaving me standing alone in the center of the hall. All the wounded are watching me.

Keep on going back to your place, don't lift your eyes, just a few more steps to your corner, ignore all the wounded looking at you. They must be whispering to each other and pitying you. Just a few more steps.

I'll wait quietly in my bed, just as Audrey wants me to, and I'll read in my book as Audrey wants, and I won't be in pain as Audrey wants. Just a few more steps, just another month of waiting for the ship.

When I get to my corner, I firmly hold the scissors still in my hand and mark a line on the plaster of my wall. Tomorrow I will mark another, just as she wants.

"John, do you hear? They don't want me. Without my leg I'm unneeded," I tell him as I sit on my bed and hold the book. "They want me to lie here in bed next to you and wait for the ship to take me home. They want me to be crippled at home. "Do you think a disabled woman like me can dance and kiss?" I keep talking to him, and thumb through the book pages for no reason. "I don't want to be a rag doll," I close the book.

It takes me a while to find the Italian cleaner who curses everyone, but finally, when I go out into the garden, I see her walking among the wounded in her black dress. She passes between them and hands them glasses of sweet juice made of synthetic orange-flavored powder.

"I want to help you." I approach her, but she walks away from me to the next wounded soldier sitting in a white garden chair, looking over the cliff to the sea.

"I want to help you." I follow her, but she just looks at me for a moment and walks to the next wounded soldier. Maybe she didn't understand me.

Without asking her, I begin to move between the wounded ones sitting in the garden chairs, taking the empty glasses from their hands. It seems they only hand them to me out of surprise, and I hobble on my crutches and chase the Italian.

"Please take them." I place two empty glasses on the tray she's holding. I can't take more than two glasses, and even then, I'm panting from the effort of chasing her through the large garden, my healthy leg still sore. My amputated leg bothers me too, but I won't give up.

"Please take them," I say to her again, giving her another two empty glasses, but she keeps ignoring me and continues to walk among the wounded. I won't break, not now, I'll have enough breaking moments at night in front of my wall, when the pain arrives and everyone is asleep, I'm scared of the night.

Again and again, I hobble between the wounded men sitting in their white chairs and enjoying the sun, taking empty glasses of juice from their hands and turning to look for her, but suddenly she's not there.

The garden is full of wounded men sitting in white deckchairs, and two nurses bend over and hold one of them, trying to help him walk, but when I look around I see no woman in a black dress walking around carrying a tray in her hand. I start to move between the wounded soldiers, searching for her, but she's gone, and finally I throw the empty glasses I'm holding onto the grass, I have no strength to keep carrying them. But I keep on searching for her. I don't want to go back to my corner, to let Audrey see that I'm resting. I am a nurse.

At the end of the garden, I notice the edge of black fabric behind the old shed, and when I get closer, I see her.

She's sitting on the ground by the old shed wall, where I was sitting that day when I ran away, wiping her cheeks and not noticing that I'm standing there watching her.

I take a few steps forward, debating whether to tell her anything, but then she notices my presence and looks at me as if expecting me to say something, her eyes red from crying.

"Thank you for helping me then, when I tried to go down the stairs, and with the bed that night." I approach her slowly, but she keeps looking at me with her black eyes and says nothing. I don't think she understands me at all. I take one step closer.

"Thanks," I tell her again, and she answers me in Italian and wipes her eyes. Maybe she's cursing me like Audrey said she used to do, and after a moment of silence where we examine each other, I turn my back to her and start hobbling to the garden. She doesn't understand me anyway.

"I hate you all. You are the same as them," I hear her tell me in English with an Italian accent.

"I just wanted to thank you." I turn to her.

"I hate you all. You are the same as them," she repeats, wiping her red eyes again.

"What do you mean, the same?"

"You Americans, you're just like the Germans." She begins to speak English in her Italian accent and doesn't stop. "Why did you have to come here from New York to my village? Don't you have enough country of your own?"

For a moment, I want to tell her that I'm not from New York, but from Chicago, but she doesn't stop talking, and it seems to me that she is speaking more to herself than to me.

"Of all the villages in the world, why did you have come to mine and destroy it? You and your soldiers and your tanks and your planes, you come and occupy and destroy our houses, and take for yourself what is left and plant your flag, as if everything here belongs to you. You are just like them." She keeps on talking and wiping her tears.

"We are different," I try to explain to her. "We're not like them."

"Yes, you are different." She looks at me with her eyes black and red from crying. "They said danke and achtung, and you say thank you. You just think you're different. The only difference between you and the Germans is you have better cigarettes." She finishes talking, wipes her teary cheeks, and turns her eyes away from me, looking at the cypress trees surrounding the hidden corner behind the shed.

I want to answer, to explain to her that she is wrong and that we've come to free them, and I approach and stand over her, hearing her quiet sobs even though she's looking away from me.

She's about my age, maybe two or three years older, and has long black hair and light brown skin, tanned from the local sun, and her fingers tremble when she wipes her eyes.

"Cigarette?" I take the box of cigarettes I'd received from Audrey out of my pocket and hand it to her. She takes one without saying a word, looking at me for just a moment with her dark eyes, before she lit it and turning her gaze to the treetops.

And I carefully lean the crutches on the wall and sit on the ground next to her, watching as she lights her cigarette and smokes in silence, and we both examine the smoke curling in the air. I have no idea what she's thinking as the tears continue dripping down her cheeks.

"Francesca," she says after a while.

"Grace," I answer.

"It's my job, not yours, don't take my job," she says when she finishes her cigarette, throws it on the dry ground, wipes her eyes, and gets up.

"I want to help you," I say, but she doesn't answer me and walks away.

I look around at the dark green trees and the mountains on the horizon, hearing the wounded talking in the garden behind the shed. I won't continue to sit here waiting for the evenings and nights to come, even if she doesn't want me to help her. I've run out of other options. No one else wants me anyway.

I start to get up, trying to support myself, and reach for the crutches leaning against the wall. But when I try to grab the wooden sticks, I slip and fall, hitting the ground.

Breathe, breathe, breathe. I'm trying to stifle the scream of pain that emerges from my mouth, tucking my lips in the dirt and whimpering hoarsely into the hard ground. My aching hand that stopped the fall gropes and feels my injured leg, examining whether it has been damaged.

Just keep breathing. I slowly lift my head off the ground, looking around. Did anyone see me fall? Does anyone pity me?

I can still hear the wounded talking in the garden, and no one is coming to help me. At least no one saw what happened, the Italian woman who walked away also didn't hear my scream. I just have to ignore what happened, it didn't happen, no one sees the tears. My nails scratch my knees and thighs again, gently touching my amputated leg. I must stop crying.

It takes time for me to sit back and lean against the shed wall, and it takes time to clean my mouth and lips from the dirt and dry leaves, and it takes time for me to take the cigarette box out of my hospital shirt pocket and tuck a cigarette between my lips with my shaking hand.

But I have no matches or lighter, and I stay seated, leaning against the wall with the unlit cigarette between my lips, feeling the smell of tobacco while my fingers crumble the plaster of the old shed wall. What will I do when I fall like this next time, and everyone sees and pities me?

Only when the sun starts setting, and the wounded are escorted into the building by the nurses, do I rise of my hiding place and walk among them, looking at the grass, careful not to slip again, raising my head every few steps and smiling at them.

"See you tomorrow," I say to Francesca, but she doesn't answer me.

I'll go back to my corner and clean myself, and I'll swallow the aspirin pills that don't help me again. And I again I won't sleep at night and read from Audrey's book to silent John, and tomorrow I'll again look for the Italian who hates me, running after her with empty glasses of orange juice.

Step by step, I cross the aisle between the beds of the wounded, my eyes on the floor, counting steps and trying to remember the last page I'd read yesterday, but when I get to our corner and sit on my bed, I see there's a bundle of letters on our locker, tied with a thin, coarse rope. No one has ever sent me letters.

4. A Bundle of Letters

I gently hold the bundle of yellow letters, inspecting the army stamps and addresses covering them before I turn the package around. Who sent me letters? But when I look at the name on the first envelope, I see they're not for me, they were written to silent John. I place them back on the metal locker standing between us, and go back to lie in my bed, turning my back to him.

But after a while, I turn from my wall and hold them in my hand again, feeling the thin paper and imagining they are mine. Since leaving home, I haven't received any letters, and I know I won't receive any either. No one from home would write to me, certainly not my mother or father, and I have no one else waiting for me. My mom works from dawn to dusk as a saleswoman in a clothing shop, coming home after sunset, preparing food for Dad, tidying up the house and going to bed. And my dad barely works and just goes out to the neighborhood bar every night with his Polish friends, drinking beer and cursing the Nazis. When he's home, he just sits next to the radio and listens to the evening news broadcasting the battles, cursing the Nazis. At the beginning of the war, he prepared a large map of Europe, ready to mark the liberation of Poland with small pennants; but after the Germans invaded Russia and the whole map was filled with small Nazi pennants marking their progress toward Moscow and Stalingrad, the map disappeared from our living room one day, though the cursing remained. I smell the letters I'm holding tightly in my hand, bringing them closer to my chest and imagining that they're mine, even though they're his. They have a faint and pleasant smell of flowers.

"I see you've received some letters, won't you open and read them?"
I open my eyes and see Audrey standing next to me. How long has she been there?

"I'll open them soon. I'm resting now."

"You must have been waiting for them for a long time."

"Yes, I was waiting for them for a long time." I hold them tightly, hiding his name with my palm.

"Who's it from?" She smiles. "Do you have someone waiting for you at home?"

What should I answer her? Shall I tell her that back home, when I went to all those dance clubs, I didn't find the one I wanted, and now it's too late? Shall I tell her how they used to compliment me on my fashionable curly hair, like in the magazines, and now no one will compliment me anymore?

"I have someone at home," I say quietly.

"You didn't tell me that," she touches my arm and smiles. "Now you have a reason to recover and go home."

"Yes, I have a reason to go home." I try to smile at her. Why am I not telling her the truth?

"You should tell me about him someday." She turns her back to me and starts taking care of John, changing his bandages. "Do you hear, John? Our Gracie has someone waiting for her at home." I hurry to tuck the letters under my pillow. He doesn't care anyway, he's barely alive.

At night, when the hall is quiet and dark, and the pain in my leg comes back, I take out the letters from under my pillow and examine them, but it's too dark.

"John, can I borrow your lighter?"

He doesn't answer me.

My fingers rummage through his bag, and I pull out the lighter, light the candle, feeling the engraving on the metal lighter again with the tip of my finger. In the dim light of the candle, I can't see what's written.

"Thank you, John," I whisper to him, examining the bundle of letters, even though I know they belong to him and that I shouldn't do it.

The yellowish envelopes are dirty with dust and mud, but I can read the name John Miller in round handwriting.

"John Miller, nice to know, your name is John Miller." I stroke his lips and wet them with a bit of water, feeling his quiet breathing.

"Who's writing to you?" I ask him after a while, still looking at the package, even though I know he won't answer me. My fingers turn the envelopes over and look for the answer, but I must untie the thread binding them to see. Only his name is visible, and a stamp with sloppy handwriting in it: Military mail, Tunisia, Third Division, transfer to Italy.

"John, may I untie the thread?"

My fingers gently untie the knot, and the letters spread over my bed's white sheet. I take the last one, holding it in my hand and examining the stamp.

"Let's see," I speak to him. "Do you know someone wrote you a letter half a year ago? Where were you at that time? In Tunisia? I'm sure it's a woman, according to the round and neat handwriting, even though I haven't opened it, it's yours. Why didn't you receive it when you were in Tunisia?"

I try to imagine him in uniform, walking in the desert in all those places that barely made headlines at home. When I was still in Chicago and went to the cinema, they would show those places in the news once in a while, before the film. "Our brave soldiers," the announcer enthusiastically described the American soldiers fighting the Germans, "in Kasserine Pass, Marrakech, Casablanca," he'd say the foreign names.

I try to remember other places he mentioned, and failed.

"I was so jealous of those newsreels," I keep talking to John. "I also wanted to fight for our nation. The soldiers always seemed smiling and happy, unlike my parents at home. Did you smile at the movie cameras when you walked in the desert?"

I move slightly away from his bed and lean back in mine, looking at him. "What's your height?" I think he's much taller than me, but I'm not sure, I've never seen him standing. I pull back the blanket covering him, only for a moment, and examine him in the dark. He's taller than me, I mustn't do that.

"I apologize. I just wanted to know." I cover him again, arrange the blanket, and stroke his hair. I have to return the letters to him, they're not mine, but I need to imagine there's someone who loves me at home, just for a few more moments.

I wet his lips with some water and wet mine too, I'm not used to talking so much, even though he's just listening and saying nothing. I turn the envelope over, in a moment it'll no longer be mine, and I wonder about all the hands and mailbags it went through until it arrived in Italy and into my hands. It's time to say goodbye to my momentary letter. It belongs to silent John. I'm not allowed to view his personal belongings.

"Well, her name is Georgia, she lives in New York State, and she wrote you a letter. Are you from New York State, too?" I ask him, but he stays quiet and doesn't tell me if Georgia is the name of the woman waiting for him at home, or maybe his mother, or anyone else at all.

For a moment I hear the nurse on the night shift walking around the hall, and I stop talking to John, hiding the letters under the pillow, not wanting her to start asking me about them.

"What did Georgia write to you six months ago, when you were in North Africa?" I ask him after the nurse walks away, returning to her bright room at the end of the hall. "Aren't you curious to know? What's on your mind when you lie there with your eyes covered? Do you also feel alone? Or do you feel comfortable in the warm cloud of morphine and the knowledge that there's someone at home who loves you?"

I hold the letter in front of the candlelight, trying to see what's written inside the closed envelope. But I can't read anything, and the mud stains on the paper also interfere, though I try to gently remove them with my fingernails. Would he like to know? Would I want someone to read me the letter if I were in his place?

"John, would you like me to read you one of the letters, or read to you from the book? Which do you prefer?"

At first I go back to the book, trying to read it to him, but as I read it in a whisper, my eyes pass the same line over and over again until I finally put the book aside and take the first letter. Just one letter.

I gently open the envelope and start reading the long lines written in curly handwriting.

"My John,

It was snowing this week, and our school's basketball court was covered in white flakes, making it look like a soft white blanket waiting for us to walk and chase each other, as we did the winter before the war, that time that you kissed my frozen nose..."

I stop reading, look at the bottom of the letter for the signature, then look back at John, who listens to me in silence.

"Well then, Georgia is probably your girlfriend. I don't know yet, because I haven't read the whole letter, but you kissed her nose when you ran after each other in the snow."

I must not continue to read him the letter. This is his love, not the love of a crippled woman who happens to be next to him right now, doing something she shouldn't be doing. Still, I can't stop reading, and my lips whisper to him all the words written in the letter, until I finish with Georgia's kisses. He must be glad I read to him. If I were in his place, I would be happy if he'd read to me.

"That's it, that's the letter from Georgia who loves you, but there's more." I gently fold the paper and return it to the envelope, tucking the whole pile of letters under my pillow, even though they're not mine. I lie down in my bed and look at the dark ceiling.

"Tell me, John, what does she look like? Is she nice?" I can't fall asleep. "Maybe you have a picture of her?" I ask after a while.

I reach out and grope for his leather bag in the dark, and rummage through its pockets until I feel the hard paper of a picture, pulling it out, lighting the candle again and looking at her.

Georgia 1941 is written on the back of the picture in her curly handwriting, and when I turn it over, she smiles at me. She has short blonde hair, slightly curly and fashionable. I also had curly and fashionable hair, but brown, not golden like hers. And she has green or blue eyes, I can't tell in the black and white photo, not dark like mine; and she's wearing a floral summer dress rather than an ugly hospital uniform. She smiles at John, who probably was the one photographing her leaning against a tree in a field full of weeds and bushes, where they lived, or maybe they went hiking before Pearl Harbor happened and it all started.

"You're lucky she loves you. You're lucky to have her," I whisper to him after returning the picture to his bag in the locker, but not before I smell it. The hard yellow paper of the picture no longer smells of flowery perfume.

I then fill my mouth with aspirin pills, blow out the candle, turn my back to John, and stroke the wall with my fingers, looking with my fingernails for more pieces I can peel. I hope the aspirin overcomes the pain tonight and I can fall asleep. And I hope someday someone will love me like that too.

The next morning I mark another line on my wall, even though I've decided not to do it anymore. I also hide John's letters in my bag, even though they are his. Then I pick up my ugly crutches and walk away from my corner filled with silent John and the picture of Georgia who loves him. I'm glad I told Audrey that I have someone, at least she won't feel sorry for me.

Bag, bag, bag, bag, my crutches hit the floor as I lower my gaze while walking through the hall among the wounded. Thirty-eight steps from side to side, I counted them yesterday. I have to raise my head so they won't feel sorry for me, but what if I don't pay attention, slip and fall? I deserve to fall. I'm a liar who reads letters that aren't hers. I deserve nothing more than working as an assistant to the cursing Italian.

And so the next day passes, and the next few. Every morning I mark another line, and every afternoon I chase after Francesca, holding empty glasses of synthetic orange juice, and every evening I read John a letter from the package sent by the woman he loves. And every night I swallow aspirin pills and sigh in pain in the dark.

John remains silent, and there are days I read him letters I've read to him before, choosing the parts I like most and trying not to stain the thin paper with my tears, ruining Georgia's curly handwriting, so I can read them next time as well. It seems to me there are parts I already know by heart.

And Francesca still ignores me, even though she lets me put empty juice cups on the tray she carries while walking through the garden in her black dress. And Audrey lets me bandage myself every morning, placing the bandages and sulfa powder on the metal locker before she goes to treat the other wounded men. This is the closest I'll ever get to being a nurse. I have to do more.

"John, do you hear?" I whisper to him at night when I finish reading one of the letters, folding it back up and returning it to the envelope. "Do you mind if I touch you?"

I wait a moment for him to respond, but he doesn't answer me, and I make sure the curtain is drawn, separating us from the other wounded before I pull back his blanket, examining the bandages and his breathing.

"I'm going to start here." I whisper to him. "Tell me if I'm doing something wrong." I carefully remove his bandage, setting it aside, and bring his lighter closer to his body so I can examine the wounds on his chest. I'd made sure to wash my hands thoroughly beforehand.

"Now tell me if this hurts you." I sprinkle the disinfecting sulfa powder on his body from the jar Audrey left this morning for my wounds.

"I think it's okay. You're not complaining." I open the clean bandages she'd left for me and start dressing his body. If I want to succeed at being a nurse, I have to practice. I'll change a bandage myself every few days.

"I think I did a good job." I run the lighter close to his body, checking the bandages I've placed and smiling at him. "I'm a nurse." I bring my lips closer to his, imagining I'm the good nurse from the movie, the one I saw then in the Chicago movie theater before the war started. But I don't kiss him, just hold my lips tightly and close my eyes despite the darkness, imagining the touch. He's not mine, he has a woman who loves him at home.

"Good night, John," I whisper to him as I return to my bed and cover myself, swallowing my aspirin pills. "Tomorrow I'll read you a letter and replace your bandages again."

"Your injury is getting better, the bandages are really clean," Audrey smiles at him the next day as I follow her with my gaze. My injured leg bothers me, but I'll get over it. Will she notice that I treated him?

"I'm glad you have less infection," she strokes his hair after she finishes cutting off the night's bandages and throwing them to the floor, waving for Francesca to come pick them up. But Francesca continues to clean among the wounded on the other side of the hall, turning her back to Audrey and ignoring her sign.

"Grace, please call the Italian to come clean here."

"One moment, I'll just finish getting dressed." I turn my back to her, opening and closing my pajama buttons.

"I don't know why we hired her. She's an ignorant Italian who doesn't know English at all. How do you even talk to her?"

"Maybe she needed a job."

"She should look for work elsewhere, not with us."

"But they're under our occupation, we need to take care of them, don't we?"

"Have you been to North Africa?" She stops taking care of John and comes to stand in front of me.

"No." I look up at her, continuing to hold onto the buttons of my open shirt.

"If you'd been in North Africa, you wouldn't feel sorry for them or think we should take care of them. I saw what they're capable of doing."

"Who, the Italians?"

"No, the Germans."

"But she's Italian." I keep looking at her and finish closing my shirt, wanting her to move so I can take my crutches.

"They fought side by side with the Germans, they're just like them." She throws my bandages onto my bed. "If you'd been in Tunisia and seen their planes bombing convoys of trucks, your opinion would be different." She puts the sulfa jar in my hand. "You think the plane that wounded you was an American plane? And the soldier who wounded John? And all the others here?"

"Yeah, you're right." I stand on my leg, jumping and pushing myself between her and the wall, taking my crutches. "I hate her as much as you do, but I have no other choice. She's the only one who lets me be with her." I turn my back on Audrey and start hobbling around the hall looking for Francesca, or the ignorant and cursing Italian as Audrey calls her.

***

"We didn't intend to destroy your village. It must have been a mistake," I tell Francesca later that day when I see her go to the corner behind the old warehouse. I wait a few moments, then follow her.

The pleasant morning sun is warming the garden full of the

wounded, who sit in their white chairs waiting to recover, and for the ship that must be already on its way here to take us home. At least that's what the lines on my wall tell me.

"You Americans never mean to." She moves her gaze away from me to the blue sea on the horizon, and sits down on the ground, leaning against the wall.

I look at her and stay standing, afraid to sit and fall like last time.

"Did someone destroy your New York?" she continues speaking to the sea.

I look at her fingers, seeing them peel off the plaster of the warehouse wall, crumbling it and throwing the reddish powder on the dry ground.

"No, no one destroyed New York."

"Have you been to my village?" She peels another piece from the wall.

"No, I haven't been to your village. I haven't had the time yet." I try to imagine her village. I have to sit next to her. I carefully support myself on my crutches and get down on my knees, removing the dry leaves, sitting down carefully and leaning against the wall.

"Once, before the war, there was a movie theater in the center of the village. We used to go there every Saturday evening to see a movie. Now there is empty sky, a gift from a German bomber."

"I'm sorry," I answer, thinking of the ruined houses in Naples that I'd seen then, the first day I landed in Italy.

"And of the square and the fountain, where we used to drink water when I was a child, only stones remain. I don't know whose gift that was," she continues to speak in her Italian accent.

"I'm sorry." I don't know what else to tell her.

"No, you're not really sorry. You live here in this mansion you took for yourself when you arrived. You made a little America here, with an American flag and American food, and American music played on a turntable you brought from America or found in an abandoned house. You don't care about my village and my fountain. But at night you send letters back home to intact New York. I'm in Italy. It's so beautiful here."

I search for something to tell her while my fingers stroke the envelopes tucked in my shirt pocket. I need to return them to John, they're his. I couldn't resist and took them with me, even though I shouldn't have.

"Do you have a cigarette?" she asks me after a while, and I give her one.

"Someday I'll come visit your village," I finally say to her after a long silence, feeling the stone wall at my back and looking for a piece of plaster to peel.

"Yes, one day you'll come visit my village, and one day you won't conquer us anymore, and one day my husband will return from the war in Russia," she answers, and it seems to me she's wiping away a tear. "Do you have another cigarette?"

***

Again she finishes smoking the cigarette I gave her and says something in Italian, getting up and returning to the garden. This time I don't try to get up and chase after her, but stay seated and follow her with my eyes, peeking at her from behind the warehouse wall. Why didn't I think she was married?

She walks among the wounded and her black dress flutters with each step she takes, and I try to imagine her holding the hand of the man she loves as they'd walk hand in hand in the village square, where I've never been. How do you feel when you love a man? Should I have asked about him?

"It has nothing to do with me. She's just an Italian cleaner," I whisper to myself, rising cautiously and starting to follow her among the wounded, smiling at them, ignoring the sweat and pain of walking with my ugly crutches. Soon the day will end, and I can return to my corner.

"Grace, do you want to join us and come to the pilots' club?" One of the nurses asks.

"But how will she dance?" Audrey asks her.

"Yeah, you're right," she replies,

"it's a pity you can't join us, you'd probably enjoy it."

"Yeah, it is a pity," I answer, turning around and hobbling away from them, looking down so I don't fall.

"At least you have someone waiting for you at home." I can still hear Audrey.

"Does she have someone at home? She's lucky, especially if he's already proposed to her," I hear the other nurse.

"I wonder if she's already written to him about her injury," Audrey answers her.

Bag, bag, bag, bag, bag, bag, thirty-eight steps across the hall to my corner, with downcast eyes, so I can lie in bed and look at the wall. I was fooled by small gossip between the nurses.

"John, do you hear?" I read him one of the letters late at night, after I've finished changing his bandages, holding the thin paper close to the dim light of the candle flame.

"She loves you, and she misses you, waiting for you to return home." I open another letter, reading her words of longing and feeling so sad.

"She asks why no letters have arrived from you. She looks at your picture every night, she keeps it in a drawer next to her dresser." I read him the following letter, written last fall. "It's raining again, and she was walking alone on the street, thinking of you." I wipe away a tear.

"John, are you asleep? Or will I keep reading you another letter?" I stroke his black hair, even though it belongs to Georgia. Maybe he'll imagine she's the one stroking his hair.

"She says there's a new teaching staff at school this year, and that there are almost no men left in town. Is she a teacher? She also writes that almost all the men have been drafted into the army, like you. And there are only two male teachers in the whole teaching staff, and she misses you so much. Why didn't you write to her?

"Was the ship carrying your letters sunk in the Atlantic by a German submarine?" I take a short break to sip from his glass of water. "What happened? Why did you let her miss so much?"

I start to feel the pain in my leg, and I open my box of pills, filling my palm and swallowing them, grimacing at the bitter taste.

"Shall I keep reading you?" I ask him, but then I hear a noise from the hall entrance and look up. Some nurses noisily enter the quiet, dark hall and approach the nurses' station, filling it with sounds of laughter, and it seems that they're a little drunk.

"They've come back from the pilots," I whisper to him. "There's a military bomber airfield nearby, behind the hill, and they invite the nurses to come visit them at the squadron's club. They say the pilots are handsome. It's nice to meet like that, but it doesn't matter to me. Who would like to meet me the way I am?"

The sounds of laughter from the nurses' station increase, even though the nurse on duty is trying to silence them.

"John, it seems to me that I'll continue to read to you tomorrow." I reach my hand out in his direction and stroke his lips.

"Please continue," I hear him whisper, his voice barely heard. But his lips move, and in surprise I blow out the candle and drop the letter on the floor.

***

5. John

"Where am I?" I hear him whisper in the dark.

I have to call the nurses, tell them he woke up. I get out of bed as quietly as I can, holding its iron frame so as not to fall, and fumble on the floor with my fingers, searching for the letter I'd dropped.

"Where am I?" he whispers again. That's not my job. I get up and place the folded letter under my pillow, careful not to make any noise. I didn't know he was listening to everything I'd said and read to him. How long has he been listening to me for?

"In a U.S. Army hospital south of Rome."

"Nurse," his lips slowly move. I look at the light coming from the nurses' station; they're still laughing with each other, probably talking about the pilots.

"Yes, I'm here," I finally answer him.

"How long have I been here?" He speaks slowly, barely mouthing the words.

"A few days." I wet his lips with my fingers after placing them in the glass of water on the locker.

"Thanks," he whispers.

"You need to rest."

"Have we taken the damned Florence yet?"

"Yes, we've taken the damned

Florence," I quietly answer, and it seems to me that he smiles in the dark when he hears my answer.

"And you're the nurse who takes care of me and reads to me?"

What should I answer? I look towards the nurses' station again, and the nurses making noise. I have to call one of them.

"Yes, I'm the nurse who takes care of you," I whisper to him.

"It's very dark here. I can't see anything."

"Yes, you were injured. You need to rest. Don't speak now."

"Will you read me more?"

"Yes, I'll sit next to you and read to you, now rest." I stroke his hair and lean into his backpack, rummaging in his front pocket, looking for his lighter to light the candle again.

Now that he's alive, I allow myself to read the engraved inscription on the brass lighter by the light of the candle: Third Division, to Hell and Back.

"You've got a long way back," I whisper to myself as I open another letter from the bundle.

"What did you say?" I hear him.

"My beloved John, I miss you so much," I start reading him the letter from the woman who loves him and is waiting for him to come home.

***

"Good morning, how are you?" I open my eyes and look at my wall, hearing Audrey by my side, but she's not talking to me.

"We were worried about you. How are you feeling?" I keep hearing her.

"I'm in pain."

"You were injured. You are now in a hospital south of Rome. You need to recover. It's going to take time. I'm Audrey, the nurse taking care of you." I roll over in bed and look at them, her hand stroking his black hair while she smiles at him.

"I know, you've already told me, but you have a different voice," he whispers to her, and I turn back to my faithful wall again.

"What do you mean?"

"When you read to me, you had a different, more pleasant voice." I smile at the wall.

"I didn't read to you."

"Some nurse read letters to me."

"You must have dreamed it. You were badly injured. There was no other nurse here who took care of you," she tells him, and I sit up. I have to get away from here before she figures out who's calling herself a nurse. My hands hold my crutches as I quietly walk away from them. I'll come back later, after she leaves.

"There's just a wounded woman lying next to you, but she's not a nurse, she's just a wounded woman." I can still hear her.

Bag, bag, bag, bag, I keep hobbling

on the hated crutches, my new legs forever, bag, bag, bag, bag.

"Are you the one who read my letters?" he whispers to me at night as I sit down in bed and rummage through his bag, looking for his lighter. What should I answer? Maybe he'll believe I was a dream?

"Yes, it's me," I answer him after a while.

"Thanks."

"It was nothing," I look down at my missing leg, forgetting that it's dark and he can't see anyway.

"Why did you read to me?" he asks after a while.

"Because you were alone in the dark."

"It's dark here," he says, as if to himself. "Sometimes painful, sometimes pleasant." I want to stroke his hair and tell him not to get used to the pleasant morphine, but I know I mustn't, I'm not a nurse anymore and I don't have the privilege to stroke his hair. He also has a loving Georgia waiting for him at home.

"So you're lying here by my side?" he asks.

"Yes."

"How were you injured?"

"A minor injury. I'll recover soon." I don't want him to feel sorry for me. The pitying looks of the nurses and the other wounded are bad enough.

"And you wanted to be a nurse too? The other nurse told me when she replaced my bandages."

"I was an intern." I play with his lighter, flicking it on and off, enjoying the sound of the metal closing on the flame.

"An intern in this war is a nurse," he whispers.

"Yeah, isn't that ironic? A nurse gets injured instead of taking care of other injuries?"

"Yes, this war is full of irony." I notice his smile as he slowly turns his face towards me. "What is your name?"

"Grace."

"Nice name."

"Thanks," I answer, and shed a tear. But it's because of the pain in my leg.

"I didn't introduce myself. I'm John." He moves his fingers slightly while his hand rests on the white bed.

"Nice to meet you, John." I touch his fingers.

"Will you read me more letters? Or dreams, as the other nurse said?"

"I've read you all the letters you got."

"Then we'll have to wait for a new letter to arrive."

"Yes, we'll have to wait for a new letter to arrive. I can read to you from a book I have here."

"Grace?"

"Yes, John."

"Can you read to me from the book you have?"

"Yes," I smile to myself.

"I like reading books. Soon I'll recover and go home. It seems the war is over for me."

"Yes, the war is over for you," I whisper to him and open the book, reading to him by candlelight, not wanting to tell him that for him, the war has only just begun.

***

"Grace. Grace," I hear him sigh.

"Yes, John," I open my eyes and turn in his direction. I can see his silhouette in the dark.

"Grace, are you here? I'm in pain." He sighs again.

"Where does it hurt?" I sit up, leaning close to him. The hall is quiet tonight.

"Everything, the wounds, they hurt."

"Try to describe to me where it hurts."

"Waves," he sighs, "all over my body." I touch his fingers and he closes them tightly, holding my hand.

"Have you received any painkillers today?"

"A long time ago, the other nurse gave me a shot, Grace, I'm in pain. Please help me."

"I'm not allowed to give you painkillers. Only she takes care of you. I'll go call her."

"Thanks," I hear him sigh again, and I get out of bed, grabbing my crutches and crossing the quiet hall, walking towards the light emerging from the nurses' station.

"Grace, why are you awake at such an hour?" Audrey asks me, looking up from the newspaper she's reading.

"It's the wounded man next to me, John, the blind man. He's complaining of pain, he's asking for a shot of morphine."

"Is he complaining and wants morphine, or are you the one who wants the morphine?" She smiles at me.

"John." I look at her.

"And you don't want a shot too? I remember you're in pain as well."

"No, I'm not in pain at all. I don't need the morphine," I answer, looking down to my missing leg, wanting just one shot so much.

"Okay." She gets up and walks to the medicine cabinet behind her, unlocking it and handing me a small glass vial and a syringe. I haven't held one like this in so long.

"Here you go, inject him. You were an intern, you should know how to do it." She sits back in her chair and takes the newspaper.

"But you have to inject him, not me." I hold the vial in my trembling hand until I'm afraid it will fall and shatter.

"I trust you." She doesn't even look up from the newspaper. "I don't hate you as you might think."

Thirty-eight steps through the dark and quiet hall to my corner and to John. I'm careful not to drop the vial and syringe in my hand. All I need is to stop for a moment and inject myself. He wouldn't know. No one would know. I'd inject half for myself and half for him, he wouldn't notice the difference, and I'm in pain too. The terrible pain was just waiting for this time to emerge, asking for the morphine itself.

"Nurse?" John asks me as I stand by my bed.

"It's me, Grace."

"Is she coming?" he moans.

"She's coming soon."

"Thanks."

"Try to fall asleep in the meantime."

"I'll try," he sighs again, his fingers clenching into fists.

Don't think, don't think, take the syringe, draw the material from the small vial, hold out your hand and inject. Don't think, you deserve to feel better.

"Thank you, nurse," he moans.

"Try to rest." I open the box of aspirin lying on the cupboard, trying to take a handful, but the box falls to the floor and I hear it shatter to pieces. My hands hold the iron bed tightly as I bend to the floor, searching in the dark for my pills, ignoring the shards of glass hurting my fingers. I must find my pills.

"Grace, are you okay?" I hear him.

"Yes, I'm fine," I answer, and shove two pills into my mouth. I must find more, to soothe the tremors and pains.

"John, are you still in pain?" I finally whisper to him after managing to swallow enough pills. I get back to my bed and try to bandage my injured fingers with the sleeve of my pajama shirt. I grope the metal locker, I might have leftover bandages. But he doesn't answer me, the morphine has already worked its magic and he's fallen asleep.

I'm still in pain. It'll take time for the pills to help, if at all.

"Good night, John, pleasant dreams." I wet his lips before lying in my bed and closing my eyes, trying to calm down. Even for me, the war is far from over.

***

"There are no new letters, just a newspaper." I return to our corner, holding the folded newspaper under my arm. For several days now, I've been going to the garden to work with Francesca, who refuses to talk with me about her missing husband, and after finishing my work, I pass through the nurses' station to find out if new letters are waiting there for him.

And every morning, when Audrey comes to take care of him and smiles at me as if on cue, I get out of bed and walk away, letting her treat him in private. I cross the hall with downcast eyes, ignoring the looks of all the other wounded men, returning only after she's said goodbye to him and continues to treat the rest of the injured.

Most of the bandages have been removed from his body and face, and he's already leaning back on his pillow, looking in my direction when he hears my crutches beating the floor as I return to our corner. Only his eyes remain covered in white bandages Audrey has changed for him.

"Did you go again?" he says when he hears my crutches, his hand buttoning his shirt. I notice that the shrapnel wounds on his chest are healing and slowly becoming scars, the same German cannon shell shrapnel that hit his eyes and took his sight from him.

"I don't want to embarrass you."

"Aren't you a nurse? You must have seen worse than me." He follows me with his head as I sit down on my bed.

"You're getting better every day." I smile at him, remembering after a moment that he can't see me, so I touch his fingers resting on the white sheet.

"The other nurse told me you've been here for a long time."

"Yes, my recovery is taking more time than I thought."

"I don't think she likes you."

"I think she tries to help me sometimes."

"She has a smile that doesn't like

you. Why does she hate you?"

"How can you tell? Are you listening to her smile?"

"I'm in a world of darkness and pain, what do I have left to do but listen?"

"Paris has been liberated after four years of German occupation," I read the headline to him, not wanting to keep talking about me.

John looks in my direction for a moment, as if thinking of what to say. "Four years of occupation," he finally says, "Four years waiting to be free."

"It's not over yet," I continue reading to him from the newspaper. The Germans have withdrawn from Paris, but they are reforming their lines on the Belgium border.

"It's over for the French, at least. Do you think you would've survived?"

"Survived what?"

"Four years of occupation."

I hold the newspaper, looking at a photo of the rows of American soldiers marching under the Arc de Triomphe, the masses of French people standing in the street cheering for them, and I wonder if I would have survived. How would I feel if I were a young Frenchman having to live under German occupation? What was it like to see a German soldier?

"Do you think they destroyed Paris?" I finally ask him, trying to read more in the article.

"They destroyed the bridges in

Florence," John speaks slowly. "They blew up bridge after bridge to prevent us from crossing them. They only left the oldest bridge undamaged, for some reason. Maybe they didn't have time to blow it up."

"Have you seen a German soldier up close?" I ask after a while. How afraid would I be of German soldiers if I was in Paris under Nazi occupation?

"Yes," he quietly answers.

"How was he?"

"He was the enemy. He wanted to kill me, just as I wanted to kill him."

"Well, John, let's see if we can get you out of bed." Audrey stands between us and smiles at me with her perfect red lipstick, a cue that my time with John is over, and I smile back at her and get out of bed. She'll be all over him until evening.

"Have you ever killed anyone?" I ask when the hall grows quiet at night, and Audrey says goodbye to him and walks away.

All day, as I was walking in the garden with the empty glasses, I looked at the wounded soldiers sitting in their chairs and tried to guess which of them had killed German soldiers.

"Yes, I have," he finally answers.

"And were you afraid of them?"

"You know," he speaks quietly, almost whispering, "since landing south of Rome, at Anzio, I haven't been afraid." He pauses for a moment, and then continues: "We were on our way to the beach in small landing craft, and we all knew the Germans were waiting for us. We all held our weapons tightly." I can see his fingers closing into a fist in the dark. "We waited for the boat ramp to drop, so we could start running towards the sand and the German machineguns." He stops again for a moment. "In the distance I heard cannon fire from the huge warships firing at the shore, like thunder. I heard the engine noise of our small boat struggling against the waves. We were all trembling from the cold wind over the sea, and the foam of the waves splashing into the boat. But most of all we were trembling with fear. Some soldiers vomited, some prayed silently, one soldier held the cross on his necklace and closed his eyes." He brings his hand close to his neck as if to show me, and I unwittingly touch the small silver cross around my neck while he keeps talking. "But I was just trembling with fear. Can I have some water?" he asks, and I serve him the glass, placing it in his outstretched palm. He takes a few sips.

"Thanks," he whispers, and continues: "In that fear, I looked at the morning sky turning red in the east, and I wasn't afraid anymore." He pauses, taking a few breaths, and I look at his lips by the faint light of the candle, waiting for him to continue.

"You see," he continues slowly, "I always knew that one day, in a month or year, I don't know when, but the day would come when the war would be over. And at that moment, on the small landing craft making its way to the beach, I decided that when that day arrived and I went back home, Private John Miller of the United States Army would no longer exist. There's Private John Miller, and there's me. It's not me who fights and shoots people on the beaches in Italy. It's him."

"But you were injured," I whisper to him, looking into his bandaged eyes.

"It doesn't matter, I came through the landing at Anzio and the siege, I survived the fighting near Rome, I came through the battle for Florence. I was wounded, and I'll recover, and I'll return home, and everything will return to normal. John Miller of the Third Division of the United States Army will remain here on Italian soil. He won't return home with me."

"And who will you be when you get back home?"

"I'll be who I was, John Miller, from my small town of Cold Spring in New York. Who I've always been."

"Good night, John Miller of Cold Spring, New York," I say to him when I finish reading another chapter of the book and blow out the candle. Maybe he'll dream about home tonight.

"Good night, Grace from America," he answers. "I don't even know where you're from."

"I'm not from a small town. I'm from Chicago."

"Good night, Grace from Chicago."

"Pleasant dreams about home."

"You too," he says, and I think about home. Maybe I'll dream I have both legs tonight, or that the war is over.

"The Russians are advancing in the east. They've taken tens of thousands of German POWs," I read the newspaper headlines to him the next day, after Audrey replaces his bondages and leaves. "No new letter for you, I'm sorry."

"I have patience, a letter will arrive soon." He looks in my direction.

"You'll go home soon." I try to imagine his small town.

"We'll both go home soon." He smiles at me, and I wonder if Audrey told him about my escape from the convoy last time, but I'm ashamed to ask him what she's told him about me. Soon the ship will arrive again. I can already feel it, they're starting preparations. This time they won't let me escape. I won't be the nurse I wanted to be, not here and not at home.

"Tell me something about your hometown." I try to change the subject.

"Cold Spring? There's not much to tell, one main street, with a grocery store, a barbershop, a clothing store, a shoe store, all the stores a person might need." He smiles at me. "And everyone knows everyone. Lots of trees, a river, and the train station to the big city of New York." He leans back and looks at the ceiling as if imagining the main street and the cars driving through it. "One small town, so close to the big city."

I want to ask him about Georgia, but I'm embarrassed and look back at the newspaper, examining a picture of a long column of German POWs captured by the Russians under the same headline declaring Russian victories in the east.

"I'll be back later, John." I suddenly get up and say goodbye to him, reaching my hands out for the crutches leaning against the wall. I have to do something.

"Grace?"

"Yes, John?"

"You have a lot of grace in you," he smiles at me, and I look at him and think he wouldn't have said that if he knew I was lying to him about my injury.

"Francesca," I find and call her to come with me to our corner behind the shed, pushing the newspaper into her hands once we're there, showing her the headlines.

"The Germans are withdrawing from France. Why are you showing me this?" She looks at me.

"No, the second headline, the Russians are taking German soldiers as prisoners of war."

She looks at me and doesn't seem

to understand what I want to tell her.

"Maybe your husband was also taken prisoner. Maybe he's alive."

Francesca looks at the newspaper and examines the picture for a long time. Maybe she's trying to find her husband in the huge curving column of black dots captured by the Russians, but suddenly she throws the newspaper on the ground.

"Do you think the Russians will keep them alive after what the Germans did to them in Stalingrad? Do you really think they will give the Italian prisoners food and coats for the winter, after they fought side by side with the Germans?"

"You have to believe that they will." I try to stand in front of her.

"To believe?" She looks at me angrily. "It's easy for you to tell me I have to believe, isn't it?" Her eyes blaze with rage, and the little silver cross around her neck shakes with every word she says. "And what about you? Do you believe? I heard you screaming at night when you didn't even know my name. I'd clean under your bed and hear you begging to die, or asking God to return your lost leg. I heard you cry to the nurses to give you more morphine. Do you still believe someone will let you go back to being a nurse, and not just pick up empty glasses after the Italian woman?" She takes a few steps away from me, her black hair scattering everywhere, but after a second, she turns back to me. "It's easy to tell others they have to believe in things that won't happen."

She spits on the newspaper lying on the ground, steps on it and crushes it, tearing it to pieces with her shoes. "I do not believe the Russians or the Germans," she doesn't stop talking. "And you should stop believing that your leg will grow back and that you'll be a nurse again." She starts walking away from me, spitting on the newspaper again. "I didn't tell you I have a husband who disappeared in the Russian winter so that you'd pity me. If anything, I feel sorry for you, and out of pity I let you feel you're worth something by collecting empty glasses of orange juice."

"I don't pity you, and you don't pity me," I shout back at her, but she doesn't stop walking, and I start crossing the garden behind the hospital, passing the wounded men sitting in their deck chairs and the Italian woman collecting glasses of empty orange juice from them. I don't care whether they look at me or what they think of me, the crippled woman with the crutches. I don't care what the Italian in the black dress thinks of me either. I slowly approach the edge of the cliff overlooking the sea and look down, playing with the crutches on the edge of a rock, jamming the tip of the wooden sticks into the hard stones.

The blue waves at the bottom of the cliff cheerfully shatter on the black rocks, spreading white foam around them. Below me, down the narrow path going from the cliff to the beach, I can see two off-duty nurses dressed in fashionable blue

and mustard swimwear, making
their way to the white sand.

"The sea is beautiful from here." I hear a voice and turn around, careful not to stumble.

"Yes, Head Nurse Blanche."

"Do you like the sea?"

"Yes, I do," I answer, even though I don't like it anymore. I haven't gone to the sea since arriving here. Back then, at home, packing my things for the war, I placed a swimsuit in my bag. But now it's too late.

"When do you know it's your last time?" I ask her after standing together in silence for a while.

"You never know." She keeps

looking at the horizon. "Or rather, it's for you to decide when the last time will be."

"Sometimes the war decides for you." I think of the red swimsuit I had. It was lying at the bottom of my army duffle bag, lost the day I was injured. Maybe it's better that way.

"And sometimes you decide for the war," she replies, still looking at the horizon. "There are those who aren't nurses anymore, yet they give wounded men morphine at night, or just read books to them, or help Italian women. It seems to me they're the ones deciding for the war."

"I don't think the Italian woman wants me to help her anymore." I keep looking down at the two girls who have reached the foot of the cliff and are now walking on the white sand, looking for a place to lie in the sun.

"Sometimes people are in pain even if their body looks unharmed," she says, and walks away. I follow her with my eyes and see her approach Francesca, taking a glass of orange juice from her and thanking her, gently touching her arm.

Francesca ignores me the following days as I try to help her. She proudly turns her back to me and walks among the other wounded, collecting their glasses and not smiling at anyone.

"Aren't you working with the Italian anymore?" Audrey asks me as I enter from the garden, panting and struggling with the crutches. "I thought you liked her." She smiles at me.

"No, I'm still working with her," I answer, turning towards my corner. I don't want to talk to her about Francesca.

"Right from the start, when you arrived, I knew you were the kind of person who liked them."

"Them who?" I stop and turn to her.

"Them, the Italians."

"What's wrong with liking them?"

"Do you remember that they're our enemies?"

"They're no longer our enemies, we occupied them, they've surrendered and banished Mussolini." I start hobbling away from her towards my corner.

"And do you think banishing Mussolini puts the past away? That's it, they're no longer our enemies?"

"Do you think Francesca is our enemy?" I stop walking and turn back to her.

"She surely doesn't like us."

"Yes, she doesn't like us," I quietly answer.

"They fought against our soldiers, the Italians. Now they deserve to suffer, don't you think?"

"Don't you think they've suffered enough?"

"We give her a job. I think we're doing pretty big favors for those who were shooting at us just a few months ago. I think that's more than enough."

"I don't think she ever shot at anyone. I think she's trying to survive, like the rest of us."

"It's their fault they chose to be fascists. I'm not sorry for them." She smiles at me with her red lipstick.

"I think nurses are supposed to like people."

"I think you're not a nurse, so you surely can't have an opinion about that."

"I used to be a nurse."

"No, you were an intern, now you're

a cripple waiting to go home, even though the last time you managed to escape me."

"I apologize that it was during your shift."

"It seems to me you've recovered enough if you no longer need the lovely morphine. Soon the white ship with the Red Cross will come pick you up. You'll have to return to our beloved nation and stop connecting with our enemies."

"The ship is on the way?" I take one step closer to her.

"Don't worry, it's probably on its way somewhere in the Atlantic Ocean, trying to avoid German submarines. Maybe you like them too?" Why does she hate me so much? What did I do to her?

"Maybe I like people."

"Maybe it's time for you to go home, don't you miss home?"

"Yes, I miss home," I answer, turning my back to her and walking to my corner, not telling her that I miss my leg most of all.

"Is that you, Grace? I can recognize you by the walk." He smiles at me, and I stand at a distance from him, leaning my hated crutches against the wall. At least John and the wall are blind enough not to see my missing leg.

"Yes, it's me. Sorry, there's no letter." I sit down on my bed. "Say, John, what do you miss most?" I ask, and regret the moment the words came out of my mouth. I should be more sensitive.

"It's personal." He looks in my direction.

"Don't you have something you miss that isn't personal?" I can't hold myself back, I'm tired of being so alone with my pain.

"I miss the landscape," he replies after thinking for a while, and I feel ashamed for asking.

"I miss the view of Tuscany," he speaks slowly. "The hills that gently slope towards the dirt roads, the cypresses standing tall at the sides of the fields, marking our paths." He pauses before continuing to talk: "You know, I knew we were at war and that the Germans were hiding in front of us, in battle positions, and that I should be careful. But every night, before I closed my eyes in a ditch or an abandoned house, or just lying in the field under the stars, I imagined that one day after it was all over, I'd bring her here, to show her the hills of Tuscany."

I get out of bed and walk away from him, leaning against the wall even though it's uncomfortable for me and I have to hold onto the window. But I don't like being close to him when he talks about the woman he loves.

"You should really bring her here when the war is over."

"And here? Outside the hospital, how's the view?"

"Beautiful as the hills of Tuscany," I answer, even though I've never seen the hills of Tuscany, only the ruins of Naples and the hospital tent where I worked non-stop during the attack. Since then I've been here, in this large mansion that has been turned into a hospital.

"Describe the landscape to me, I can imagine what you see."

"I'm not sure I can describe what you want to hear."

"I've heard you read me stories and letters. I'm sure I'd like your words." He gets up in bed and sits as if waiting for me to start talking.

I hold my crutches, lean on the window frame and start talking to him. "We're in a hospital by the beach, but from our window it's impossible to see the sea. The sea is on the other side," I continue describing it to him, mixing reality with my imagination. What does it matter what's outside? He can't see anyway. "From here you can see the green hills stretching towards the mountains."

"What else do you see from our window?"

"The driveway at the front of the hospital. It's beautiful and well-kept and surrounded by trees." I look at the front driveway and the military trucks parked on the side, next to a stack of fuel barrels. "At the center of the front driveway is a patch of flowers." I look at the military jeep parked near the entrance, next to the big white flag spread out on the ground with the Red Cross marked in its center.

"What kind of trees?"

"Tall, upright cypress trees, on either side of the front gate." I see the two officers leaning against the jeep next to the front steps. They both have visor caps brown leather pilot coats. "Next to each of them is a beautiful bougainvillea." They talk to two nurses in white uniforms while standing in the same indifferent pose of the self-confident officer. "The bougainvillea is close to the cypress trees, literally flapping on them and climbing between their branches, filling them with flowers."

"Georgia loves flowers."

"The bougainvillea has a strong fuchsia color." I see the two nurses laughing, probably from a joke the pilots told them.

"She loves roses the most. I used to bring her roses. Do you think there are roses here?"

"I'm sure you can get roses here. There must be a rosebush here you can pick." One of the pilots places his hand on the nurse's arm, and it seems to me that she likes his touch.

"When I recover and return home, we'll get married." I turn to him and see him smiling in my direction.

"I know she's waiting for you." My fingers caress the window frame.

"She wanted to get married before I went to war, but I didn't want to. I was afraid something would happen to me, even though I didn't tell her that."

"So what did you tell her?" I look at his bandaged eyes. Why haven't any of the nurses had the courage to tell him he'll be blind?

"I told her we'd write letters to each other, and when I returned from the war, I'd propose to her. It'll happen soon."

"Yes, it'll happen soon. The ship is on its way." I look back at the window, seeing the pilots hugging and kissing the nurses goodbye as they get into the jeep.

"She's waiting for me," I hear him whisper to himself.

"Yes, she's just waiting for you." The nurses keep standing on the front stairs, looking at the jeep driving away through the broken gate.

"I miss her smell so much. Have you ever felt such a strong longing like that?"

"No," I whisper to myself as I look at the jeep moving down the main road towards the airfield, following it with my eyes until it disappears behind the hill. I'm lame like the other nurses, I also don't have the courage to tell him he'll remain blind.

At least I can try to get him roses so he can smell the flowers of the woman he loves.

***

"Where can I get rose perfume? Or rose flowers?" I ask Francesca the next day. It took me time to stand in the corner of the garden and wait for her to go behind the shed. When I saw her disappearing behind the wall, I crossed the garden and joined her, placing my crutches on the wall and sitting next to her. This was my corner first, and if she's still angry at me, she can find another corner for herself.

"You can go look in the village. Maybe the Germans left perfume after they withdrew and took everything to their dear fraus in Berlin," she answers, looking the other way.

"Can you try to get me some?"

"I'm busy. I don't have time to help you."

"Do you think I can go to your village like this?"

"You can ask one of the nurses to go instead of you."

"I can pay you in cigarettes if you don't have time to help me."

"Do you think you can offer me cigarettes out of pity?"

"I don't pity you," I raise my voice slightly.

"You're from America. You're spreading your cigarettes all around because you're sorry for us."

"Do you think I feel sorry for you?" I burst out at her. "Don't you think I'm busy enough pitying myself? Do you think I just don't want to see your village?" I raise my voice. "Do you think it's nice for me to stand on the edge of the cliff and watch the other nurses go to the sea? Or going to visit the pilots? When all I do is look down at the floor all day so I don't stumble." She keeps looking away from me. "All you think is that I'm a spoiled American who's full of cigarettes. Here, take my cigarettes." I throw the box at her.

"Americana, I did not mean..." she whispers, and I notice that she is shedding a tear.

"Just don't you pity me." I try to get up, wanting to be alone, but when I place my hand on the wall my palm slips on the plaster, and I fall again and hit the ground. The wave of pain and offense breaks through my whole body, and I shove my face in the dirt and the dry leaves, whimpering into them.

"Americana, are you okay?" She gets up quickly and tries to hold me.

"Go away, don't pity me," I whisper to her while sobbing with my eyes closed. I can manage the pain by myself. "Leave me alone, please."

"Americana," I feel her hand touch my hair.

"Just go, please go." I keep my eyes closed and don't raise my head.

Only after I can no longer hear the rustle of leaves around me do I open my eyes and lift my face from the dirt, carefully standing up and looking around, trying to make sure no one saw me fall. I don't want anyone to feel sorry for me. My hands clean the dry leaves off my clothes as much as I can. At least I wasn't injured like last time. The squashed cigarette box was left lying on the ground, and I want to pick it up, but I'm afraid I'll slip again. I'll leave it where it is,

Francesca will probably take it next time she sits here.

Step by step, I return to the garden among the wounded, supported by my crutches and acting as if nothing happened. When I look around, I don't see Francesca, but when I enter the hall in the evening and reach my corner, there's an enamel mug standing on the locker, filled with red roses. Next to the flowers is a letter for John that someone left there.

6. Dear John

"Dear John," I begin to read the letter to him by candlelight, and only my whispered voice is heard in the dark hall.

"It's been so long since I've written to you, and frankly, it's been so long since I've received a letter from you." I stop for a moment and look at him.

"Please keep reading," John looks at me and smiles, reaching his hand out and groping for the rose in the enamel mug, holding the red flower in his hand.

"I don't know how to write..." I read quietly and stop, continuing to read the following lines without whispering the words.

"Grace, I can't hear you."

"Wait, I can't read it." I bring the paper closer to my eyes, continuing to read a few more lines.

"Is everything alright?"

"The light from the candle is too weak. I can't understand what she wrote."

"Is everything okay? I hear something different in your voice."

"No, everything's fine," I answer. "I fell in the garden today and it still hurts a little, but it's nothing." I remember at the last minute that I haven't told him about my amputated leg. "The candle's almost gone. I'm going to get a new one. Give me a few minutes." I get out of bed, my hands gripping the letter tightly.

"I'll be waiting," he replies, smelling the flower in his hand.

"Crippled Grace, what woke you up at this hour? You can't fall asleep because of pain, and you want more of my magic medicine?" Audrey asks as I approach the nurses' station, leaning against the door frame and wanting to keep reading the letter, even though I'm hiding it from her.

"No, I just can't sleep," I answer, wishing she would go for a walk among the wounded in the hall and leave me alone for a few minutes.

"I'm sorry, but this time I can only give you aspirin." She gets up to bring me some pills from the jar behind her, and I turn my gaze back to John. In the dark hall, only our candle continues to flicker in the corner. She won't leave the nurses' room.

"Thank you. I'll try to overcome my pain." I walk away from her with the pills in my hand, and sit on the stairs to the second floor, careful not to stumble, starting to reread the letter in the dim light of the lamp above my head.

Dear John,

It's been so long since I've written to you, and frankly, it's been so long since I've received a letter from you. I don't know how to write what I'm going to now. There's no easy way to say it, there's never an easy way to write such things, but I've met someone else, and we're together.

I've been waiting for you for months, for a letter that never arrived, thinking and fearing that you'd forgotten me.

The distance from you, the longing and the loneliness were unbearable for me, and he was by my side when I felt I was falling apart. And now we're together...

What shall I tell him? I look up from the letter I'm holding. It'll break him into pieces. Why couldn't she wait for him a little longer? I lower my eyes and keep reading.

When we parted, we said the war would never change us and tear us apart, but we were wrong, it's changed us, you went overseas and I found a new way... I stop reading for a moment and wipe the tears from my cheeks. Why was she doing this to him when he was so vulnerable? How would I read it to him?

I will never forget our love that has gone.

Georgia

And that's it. The letter is over. And I hold it in my trembling hands and don't know what to do. John is waiting for me. I try to breathe and think: what will I tell him?

"What happened? Is everything okay? It took you a long time," he asks when he finally hears the sound of my crutches by his bed.

"I apologize. It took the nurse on duty a long time to find me a candle."

"Is the night shift nurse the one who likes you? Audrey?" He smiles at me and keeps holding the red rose. I hate the smell of roses.

"Yes, it's her again." I smile through tears. "Give me two minutes, and I'll keep reading to you."

"Don't let her make you cry," he holds out his hand in my direction.

"Dear John..." I start reading to him again, skipping the lines I'd read before. "Summer has just started, and I continue walking through the garden every day on the way to school, looking at the roses and thinking of you..." I stop for a moment and look at him. Will he notice my trembling voice? Will he notice the words are mine and not hers? It took me a while to convince Audrey to give me a piece of paper and a pencil, and it took me a while longer to try and think of what to write for him as I walked away from her and sat on the steps again, writing to him in the dim light of the lamp.

"I've been waiting for a letter from you for so long," I keep reading. "Imagining myself opening it and reading your words... John, why didn't you write to her?" I scold him in a feigned voice, though I know it doesn't matter anymore anyway. Georgia has already made her decision.

"I wanted to write to her," he tells me in the dark, his fingers gently stroking the flower in his hand. "I would sometimes sit at night in the desert, after the sun went down, and the sky would be filled with stars and cannon fire on the horizon, and I couldn't write to her. Or in Sicily, after holding my rifle for two days, protecting a ruined building against German attacks," he continues to speak to me from the darkness, "how could I write words of love at night, after all the war I saw during the day? Georgia seemed so far away to me, living in a peaceful world full of smiles and trees and flowers." He smells the flower in his hand, and I feel the tear running down my cheek. "You see," he continues, "there were those who wrote to their loved ones, but I wanted to keep our love clean and pure from the war around me. That's what we promised each other, that our love would go on even if we didn't hear from each other, no matter what. Can you understand why I didn't write to her?"

I lower my eyes, knowing I need to tell him. But I don't have the courage.

"I'm waiting for you to get back to me. Love, Georgia." I finish reading the letter to him and fold the paper.

"Thank you, Grace from Chicago, have a good night," he whispers to me later.

"Good night, John from a small town near New York City. She's waiting for you to come home, and get married," I answer and stretched my hand out to my wall, trying to peel off as much plaster as I could. I had to tell him the truth.

***

"Who is the blind man?" John asks me a few days later, when I get to our corner and he hears the sound of my crutches.

"What does that mean?"

"Who is the blind man?"

"What do you mean?"

"Just answer me, who is the blind man?" He raises his voice slightly.

"Where did you hear that?"

"What does it matter where I heard it?" He looks in my direction, his eyes covered with white bandages. "Who is the blind man?"

"Where did you hear that?" I whisper, not wanting the other wounded men to look at us, though it seems to me that everyone is already watching us.

"From two nurses who spoke next to my bed this morning, they thought I was asleep. Who's the blind man? The nurse you like, Audrey. She said that." He follows me with his head as I step towards the window and look out at the front driveway and the ambulances parked there.

"Your vision has been damaged," I quietly say, unable to look in his direction, even though it doesn't matter, he doesn't know where I'm looking anyway.

"Yes, I was injured, but my eyesight isn't improving. You're a nurse, tell me, will I see again? All the other nurses refuse to answer me."

I am silent, looking out the window again, examining the cypress trees outside the hospital and how they bend in the autumn wind.

"Will I remain blind?" he asks quietly.

I continue to say nothing, watching the empty road to the hospital, keeping my back to him.

"I thought you were my friend," he says after a while.

"I'm trying to help you." I turn from the window and start hobbling towards his bed, supporting myself with the metal bed frame. He's so alone now, and he doesn't even know how much yet.

"Please go. I don't want you to help me."

"Please. I want to help you."

"Please go." He turns his back to me, and even though I stretch out my hand to him, I stop myself and don't stroke his hair. I mustn't do that, he thinks he has a woman waiting for him at home.

"Please."

"Just go."

I slowly hop on one leg to my crutches and start moving away from our corner, lowering my eyes and looking at the floor, feeling the other wounded men and the nurses staring while I cross the hall.

The sound of the enamel mug hitting the wall makes me cringe for a moment, but I don't turn around and keep hobbling. I hear more bumps, maybe the book being thrown at the wall or other things from our locker.

Bag, bag, bag, bag, keep walking. He's the blind one, not me. I have my own wounds to handle, and they're painful enough without thinking about the pain of others. I look at my missing leg. Why did I even start helping him? Why did I read him the letters at night? I have to get out of here, the stares from the other wounded are suffocating me.

After sitting behind the old warehouse for most of the day, and playing with the box of cigarettes left on the ground, I return to the building in the evening, hobbling on my crutches.

"I thought you wanted to be a nurse and help the wounded, not break their spirits," I hear Audrey from the nurses' station, and stand at the entrance to the hall.

"This isn't a field hospital," she keeps on talking, "or wherever you were when someone decided you might be an intern nurse. This is a place of caressing and loving hands." I turn to her, thinking of something to answer her, but she doesn't let me.

"Why exactly did you tell him he'll stay blind? Do you have the authority to say such things?"

"No, I have no authority," I answer, thinking that I had no authority, but I had the courage.

"You have no authority, nor are you a nurse, and yet you act like a nurse."

"Yes, Red Lipstick Nurse."

"You know, I feel sorry for you. You wanted so much to be a nurse, and you failed. Maybe you should stay in your corner, where you do nothing."

"Yes, Red Lipstick Nurse." I straighten my chin and look at the calendar over her head, trying to see whether the ship's arrival date is marked.

"Or busy yourself picking up dirty glasses of orange juice with the Italian you like so much, though I realize you're failing there too."

"Yes, Red Lipstick Nurse."

"And stay away from John."

"I have no intention of getting close to John. You're doing a great job taking care of him, his sight will probably return soon," I answer and turn my back to her, not waiting for her answer, leaving the hospital. I don't want to be close to him, he also probably doesn't want to be close to me.

The cold breeze blows in my face as I stand on the cliff's edge and look down at the stormy sea hitting the rocks. I can barely see the white foam in the dark.

"Why is all this happening to me?" I scream at the wind, looking back at the hospital building and hoping no one heard my screams. But the building remains quiet, and only the lit windows look at me, accusing me with their yellow eyes. Why did I even start helping him?

"I'm not guilty," I shout into the sea as I slowly walk on the slippery rocks, holding my crutches for support. "I was just trying to be nice to him, so he wouldn't hurt so much. It's not my fault they put him next to me, it's not my fault he was injured, it's not my fault everyone thought he would die. I just felt sorry for him." I keep shouting at the rocks as I take the cigarette box out of my pocket and pull out a cigarette with trembling fingers.

"What did I do wrong? Wasn't I a good nurse? Didn't I try to help him?" I ask the waves, which crash on the black rocks at the bottom of the cliff, spraying the air with sea drops carried by the wind and hitting my body where I stand at the top.

"I was just trying to be a good nurse," I yell at the sea as I light the cigarette with John's lighter, looking at the flame fighting the wind. "Just one cigarette, I won't break. All I wanted was to be good to people," I cry to the sea.

The wind keeps hitting my face and scattering my hair, but I stay on the rock, inhaling the smoke and coughing, holding John's lighter in my hand. I have to give it back to him. For a moment, I look down at the sea and touch the small cross around my neck.

"God," I whisper to the wind that strikes me. "What do I have to do? I promise to give it a try."

But the wind doesn't answer me, it just keeps blowing in my face, and I keep coughing from the bitter smoke, and when I finally head back to the building, the lit windows keep staring at me with their yellow accusing eyes.

"I'll stay away from him, I'll recover, and I'll leave this place," I whisper to the yellow windows looking at me.

***

7. Rage from the sky

"I'll stay away from him," I whisper to myself over the following days when I see him sitting on the bench in the garden, looking at the sky.

Every morning Audrey takes him outside and seats him on the same bench overlooking the gray sea, stroking his head and leaving him there. Every day he sits on the bench for hours, looking at the horizon with white bandages covering his eyes. Sometimes I see him holding a book in his hand, and once I notice him flipping through the pages, moving them aimlessly while his gaze is aimed at the horizon.

Now and then she approaches him

and puts a hand on his shoulder, whispering something in his ear and then walking away, leaving him to continue sitting in front of the autumn wind coming from the sea.

Even at night, we say nothing, I read from the book in silence, dog-ear the pages at the end of each day even though it destroys the book, and he lies there in darkness, maybe sleeping, maybe listening to the rustling pages as I read.

In the mornings I turn my back on them, hurrying as much as I can to get organized, say goodbye to the wall, get away from the corner, and go out to the garden to enjoy the autumn sun. I'm not a nurse, and I shouldn't approach him, or Audrey will complain about me.

Even today, when I look at him, he's sitting on his bench. Still later I see him going down on his knees on the grass, searching the ground with his hands, probably looking for the glass of juice that has fallen, his hands groping in all directions.

"Can you help me?" I ask him, and he raises his head.

"I don't think you need my help." He fumbles with his hands until he finds the bench and goes back to sitting on it, leaving the glass lying on the grass. "And I don't need pity."

"I don't feel sorry for you. I need help practicing with my crutches."

"There are many other wounded here who would be happy to help you. I hear them talking in the garden all day. You don't need to pity the blind."

"I miss our conversations."

"I'm a very bad conversationalist these days. It's hard for me to start small talk about the weather or the view around us."

"I thought Audrey was talking to you."

"She's just stroking my hair, as if it'll make my vision improve."

"Please help me, I miss your stories."

"I've told you all the stories I have," he answers, but he gets up and stands in front of me, and I raise my gaze and look at him. He is taller than me.

"Put your hand on my shoulder, help me walk with my crutches." I take his hand and place it on my shoulder.

"Audrey really doesn't like you."

"Yeah, she really doesn't like me. At least she just went into the building. So we have a few minutes of freedom. Help me walk, I have to practice."

"So you can run away from here?" he asks, and I cringe. Did she tell him what I did last time, when the ship arrived?

"Everything okay? Do you not like my touch?"

"Everything's fine. I like your touch."

"So why did I feel your body tense?"

"Tell me something. Tell me about Tuscany."

"Do you always change the subject when it's not right for you?"

"I miss your stories of Tuscany and the desert." I walk slowly, feeling his warm fingers on my shoulder.

"At one end of a dirt road we walked down, we came to an old oak tree. It had probably stood there for thousands of years." He quietly speaks as if wanting me to be the only one to hear him. "The thick tree trunk was wrinkled like an old man, and its green canopy cast a heavy shadow on the brown ground beneath it. As we approached it with our guns drawn, looking carefully and scanning for a German ambush, it seemed to me that it was looking at us, examining our steps, trying to see how determined we were to win this war." He continues to hold my shoulder gently. "Later that day, when we stopped to rest for a few minutes under its shadow, I thought that this tree must have seen the German soldiers before us cross the same dirt road at its feet, and the Crusaders and the Romans before that. This oak tree must have seen all that could ever be seen on Earth." John continues to tell me about the oak tree in Tuscany as we walk over to Francesca, and I place his hand on the tray so he can choose a glass of orange juice for himself.

"Tell me more," I ask, sitting next to him on the white bench overlooking the sea.

For the next few days, he waits for me in the garden with stories, and I patiently wait until Audrey disappears into the building before getting close to him, placing his hand on my shoulder or sitting next to him on the bench overlooking the sea. Sometimes I watch the seagulls flying above the waves. Still, most of the time I look at his lips as he describes the yellow North African dunes stretching like waves to the horizon, or the blue bays of the sea in Sicily, so clear you could toss a coin into the depths of the sea and dive and find it. I ask him questions, wanting him to tell me what his eyes saw before they were covered in white bandages forever.

Only at night do I keep quiet, forcing myself to sleep under the watchful eyes of Audrey, who walks through the dark hall.

"What's that noise?" I feel his fingers tighten on my shoulder one day as we walk in the garden, while he's telling me about a house in the middle of the battlefield and an old Italian lady who refused to leave it despite the bullets whistling around, explaining to them with her hands that she would not run away from anyone, certainly not from the war.

"It's okay. Those are the American bombers from the airfield beyond the hill," I answer.

"Something's wrong." I feel him tense up and stop walking.

"It's their engines."

"They don't sound like American bombers," he says, and I feel his fingers tighten on my shoulders even more until he's hurting me. I turn my gaze to the source of the noise, towards the sun, and see four black dots approaching us, growing with every second. Between their wings are glimmers of light and flashes, while the noise of their engines gets louder.

"Get down," I scream at John and release his hand holding me, pushing him towards the grass as we both fall. "Get down," I scream at him again, even though we're both already on the ground, and I hear the sharp whistles and screams around me. I also scream in pain when my injured leg hits the ground, while I lie on John and protect him. My hands cover my head as I try to make us both disappear into the ground, to escape the noise of the plane's engines that sounds like chainsaws, and the screams all around disturbed by machinegun thunder. When I raise my head for a second, I notice the black iron cross painted on the planes' gray wings, and the ugly swastika on their tails.

"Nurse." I hear screams from all over, and I look for my crutches. Where are they? They're lying on the grass a few yards away, but the wounded man shouting is closer than them. "Stay down," I shout to John, and start crawling to the groaning wounded man. I must take care of him. His pants are torn, and a stream of blood is dripping from his red leg.

"Your hand," I shout at him when I manage to reach his side. I tuck my hand against his bleeding femoral artery and place his hand on mine, pushing our fingers as hard as I can to stop the blood flow. "Hold on tight," I keep shouting even though I'm close to him and there's no need to shout. "Your belt," I struggle with my other hand to loosen his belt, pulling it with all the strength I have, and once it's loose I begin wrapping it around his wounded leg to make a tourniquet.

"A stick, I need a stick," I shout, and grope the grass for a branch, grabbing it and tightening the tourniquet. All around I hear screams and people running, and also more nurses and doctors in their white uniforms.

"Hold on and don't let go. You'll live." I place his hand on the stick tightening the belt. "Do not let go," I shout at him again, searching for the next wounded man lying still on the grass, looking at the sky and the planes that have already gone.

I manage to crawl to him, opening his shirt and trying to block the wound in his chest with a piece of cloth by ripping my shirt pocket. Then I support myself as much as I can and start resuscitating him. He can be saved. The screams around me don't stop, but I just press my lips to his and breathe as much as I can, ignoring the sweat and the noise around me.

Keep resuscitating, keep resuscitating, keep resuscitating. "Doctor," I shout, "I need a doctor here."

Keep resuscitating, keep resuscitating, keep resuscitating. "Doctor," I shout hoarsely. How long has it been? I mustn't stop. He will live.

Keep resuscitating, keep resuscitating, keep resuscitating.

"Grace, stop. He's dead." I feel a hand resting on my shoulder. "You need to stop."

"He needs a doctor, he still has a chance," I whisper.

"Grace, stop. He's dead." She keeps talking to me, and I think it's Head Nurse Blanche. Her uniform is covered in bloodstains, and she leans next to me. "Are you okay? Were you injured?"

And I just shake my head in denial, releasing my lips from the mouth of the wounded man lying on the grass, gazing at the sky with a surprised look.

"You need to go back to your place." She rises, and I hear her shout to the soldiers to come take the wounded I tried and failed to save. Where's John? He was under my care, is he okay?

I look around, but I can't see him. The garden is almost empty now, just a few upside-down white chairs and empty glasses of juice thrown on the grass, and nurses and doctors bending over a few wounded men still lying on the grass, carrying them out on stretchers to the operating rooms. All the wounded who weren't injured have disappeared, they must have been brought back into the main hall. I don't see my crutches either, someone probably picked them up.

"Where's John?" I whisper.

"Grace, we'll send someone to help you get in and clean up, you're covered in blood." One of the nurses approaches me, leaning beside me.

"Where's John?" I whisper again.

"Grace, he's fine, he's in his bed."

"Where's John?" I whisper again and again, looking up at the blue sky, now quiet.

***

"John, are you okay, were you injured?" I sit on my bed and try to get closer to him, but he turns his back to me.

"John, are you okay?"

"Did you lie on top of me? Did you try to protect me?"

"Yeah, I think that's what I did." I want to stroke his hair, but I don't think it'll be pleasant for him now.

"It's not supposed to be like that. I was supposed to protect you, not you protect me."

"But you can't see. You couldn't see them."

"That's exactly the point. I should stay here, in bed." He turns to me suddenly. "What's the point of all this?" He looks at me with his bandaged eyes.

"The point of what? You're the one who first heard them." I want to stroke his hand.

"Going out, trying to act normal. What's the point? I'm in the dark anyway, whether I'm lying in bed or sitting on a bench in the garden, waiting for you to come take me for a walk, listening to my stories out of pity. What's the difference? What's the point?"

"I don't feel sorry for you."

"You weren't injured like me. You don't know what it feels like."

"Yeah, I wasn't injured that badly." I don't want to tell him how I was injured. What does it matter now? Will it help him feel better? He needs encouragement, not to pity me.

"So what's the point?"

"There's a woman waiting for you at home, isn't that a good enough reason to recover?" I keep talking, glad I didn't tell him about the letter then. Maybe it'll be the right time later, but not now.

"Recover for her? Do I think I can recover?" I notice his trembling hands. "I've been turning my back to you every night for days, afraid you'll offer to write me a letter. What will I write her?" he asks, and I don't answer him.

"What shall I write her? 'I love you, but surprise, I'm blind'?" He leans back in his bed. "Isn't it better to be silent and not write anything? Let her think I've forgotten her, or maybe that I was killed. Maybe it's a mistake I stayed alive today, and you shouldn't have thrown me on the ground and tried to protect me. Maybe God sent them to finish the job where the German shell failed?"

"Don't talk like that. I care about you."

"You just feel sorry for a blind

wounded man sitting in bed next to you. You shouldn't have protected me. It's not your job."

Without saying a word, I grab my crutches and hobble away from him.

Bag, bag, bag, bag, thirty-eight steps to the exit and the dark garden at night, passing through the upside-down deck chairs. I make my way to the cliff overlooking the sea.

"Enough," I scream at the sea. "Enough with all this pain around me. I'm running out of strength." I sit bent over on the bench, ripping the chain with the cross from my neck and throwing it at the rocks. "How much longer can I be in pain and fail at everything I try?" I whimper as I light a cigarette in the dark, breathe in the smoke, and cough, not wiping the tears from my cheeks.

But the waves and the sea don't answer me. They're just waiting for me to jump into them, as I once wanted to when I realized I'd lost my leg. Back then, I didn't the courage.

"I need some courage," I whisper to the rock as I light another cigarette. But finally I turn around and go back to the dark building and the bright doorway looking at me mockingly. I'll try to beg the one who likes me, maybe she'll agree to give me a dose of morphine and I'll be able to fall asleep tonight. But she's not on duty, just another nurse I don't know who refuses me.

***

"Eight days, I was in Italy as a whole person for only eight days," I say to Francesca the next day. "Eight days and six months without a leg and two German plane attacks."

We both sit down to rest in our hiding place, and I take out a cigarette and light it, inhaling the smoke and feeling myself suffocate. But I don't stop smoking.

"After the first time, I stayed like that." I touch my amputated leg and exhale the smoke into the blue sky. "The first time, when I heard the airplane engine and the shooting around me, I didn't understand what was going on, what all those flashes were." My fingers play with the dry leaves.

"By the second time, I understood, but it didn't change anything."
I keep talking slowly, looking at Francesca, but she looks at the sea and says nothing.

"Eight days and two attacks, and I only lost one leg, that's not so bad, is it?" I look down, seeing her fingers also playing with the dry leaves, crushing them.

A few more minutes pass, and I light another cigarette for myself, feeling my trembling hand. I can't tell her about the flashes of the bombs hitting the ground, the air filling with dirt and a burnt smell, the screams that were all around me. The worst was the screams. They keep me awake at night as my fingernails scratch my leg, wanting to feel some pain. How much more should I suffer?

"And you know what's the worst thing?" I ask Francesca, but she's silent. "The feeling of helplessness, that I can do nothing." I take a deep breath. "And now, with these crutches, it's even worse. I depend on them and can't even try to escape." I push them with my hand and drop them to the dirt, enjoying the sound of them hitting the hard ground.

"I hate you," I turn in their direction and kick them with my single foot. "I hate you," I keep shouting, ignoring my tears. "Better to lie next to John in bed all day and look at the wall than be 'the crippled woman with the crutches,' the one everyone is always staring at when she passes through the aisle between the beds." I kick them over and over, pushing them away from me. "When will the ship arrive to take me from this bleeding place?"

***

8. Francesca.

"Wake up." I feel someone touching my shoulder, waking me up. I open my eyes and examine the new scratches on the wall in front of me.

"Wake up. Come with me." I feel the hand again. I turn around and see Francesca standing over my bed. What does she want from me?

"Come with me." She pulls me to a seating position and hands me the crutches, placing them between my arms. I refuse to take them and lie back on my bed. I have had enough in the air raid. I will stay in my bed, like John.

"Come with me." She doesn't give up and pulls me back to sit up. She hands me the crutches, placing them under my armpits and closing my palms around them. "Come with me."

"Where?" I stand up and look at John. Maybe he'll say something to her. But he is silent. After what had happened, he fell silent again.

"Where?" I ask again. I don't want to go outside to the garden with her.

"I want to show you something." She holds my arm and walks by my side as we walk down through the hall of the wounded, as if trying to make sure I don't run away from her. Doesn't she know I'm a cripple who cannot run from anything? I lower my eyes to the floor while we walk through the aisle between the other beds, but she keeps looking ahead, ignoring the men who stare at us curiously.

"Francesca, I was just looking for you. I need you to start cleaning the nurses' station." Audrey says to her as we walk past her towards the entrance.

"I will be back in a few minutes." She answers her, still holding onto my arm. "Come with me."

I walk out with her into the garden and towards our secret place behind the warehouse. She probably wants to tell me something that would cheer me up after yesterday, not realizing she would not succeed. But to my surprise, she turns onto the hospitals' front driveway, helping me go down the front steps.

"Come with me." She continues walking on the gravel, passing the big Red Cross flag spread out on the ground, walking towards the cars parked at the side near the stone wall.

I pause for a moment to look at the torn Red Cross flag. It did not protect us against the German planes. I notice that it is full of bullet holes, probably from the German machineguns; a souvenir from the airplanes that attacked us.

"Where are you going?" I shout after her.

"I want to show you something." She doesn't turn around so I follow her, hobbling carefully through the gravel, paying attention to the ground lest I slip and fall.

"What do you want to show me?" I stand next to her on the side of the front driveway. In front of us are several green army supply trucks and jeeps are parked by the fuel barrels.

"Come with me." She removes a tarpaulin cover, exposing a red motorcycle that is covered with dust and mud. She lifts the hem of her black dress, tucks the soft fabric between her thighs, and sits at the driver's seat with her legs spread, motioning for me to sit behind her.

"What is this motorcycle?"

"This is my motorcycle. Have you ever ridden a motorcycle?"

"No." I stand embarrassed beside her. Still seated, she kicks one of the pedals with her foot, and the motorcycle's engine ignites with a thunderous rattle. How can I ride a motorcycle without one leg? Doesn't she know I'm crippled now? Is she trying to make fun of me too?

"I can't go with you."

"Get up." She insists and motions for me to get closer to her. I take a step closer and place my hand on the back seat, supporting myself, as she takes the crutches from my hands. I carefully lift my amputated leg above the side of the back seat while holding it tightly. I can feel the engine shake and I'm afraid of falling.

"Hug me," She says while taking my hands and wrapping them around her waist.

What about my crutches? Will she leave them here? Where is she taking me?

Not a moment passes and Francesca places my crutches right between us. "Hold me tight." She yells over the engine's rattling noise.

"What?"

"Hold on tight." She starts driving slowly in the front driveway of the hospital. 'I hold on to her, pressing my body to her back ignoring the wooden sticks that are nestled between us.

Driving slowly, she passes the green army trucks and the jeeps standing on the siding, crossing the gate destroyed during the attack. I lower my gaze as we drive out of the hospital and onto the main road, worried that one of the nurses would see us.

"Are you alright?" She shouts after a few minutes as we drive down the road, and I can see through the trees on the sides of the road that the village houses are getting closer.

"Yes," I yell back and hold on to her a little tighter as the motorcycle shakes and jumps over the holes in the road. The road that was once well paved is now full of bumps and potholes, probably from the tanks rolling over it or the cannon shells that were fired during the fighting here. The wind on my face and the landscape around me feel so pleasant, and if only I could, I would spread my arms to the sides and imagine that I could fly like a bird, thinking of John and his stories of Tuscany.

"We're almost there." Francesca shouts to me as we approach the entrance to the village. In front of the first stone houses, on the side of the road, lies a destroyed tank. It is on its side blocking part of the road, and I can see the American white star that is painted on its turret.

My eyes follow the tank as we pass it, riding slowly through the village. I notice a group of children standing on it, playing with wooden swords.

"La vedova en moto. La vedova en moto." They shout to Francesca as we pass them.

"What were they shouting?" I ask her, but she does not answer. Maybe she did not hear me.

Inside the village, Francesca slows the motorcycle and drives down a narrow road between the houses. As we pass by a pile of bricks that was once a house, I can see the single wall that had been left standing and the seawater that is clearly visible right through the wall.

"Hold me tight." She yells to me as the motorcycle jumps over the cobblestones road, and I hug her with both my hands.

We slow down again in one of the narrow streets, driving behind a cart strapped to a donkey. Suddenly, I notice people looking at me from the balconies and entrances of their houses, their eyes examining my hospital clothes and my missing leg.

"They're looking at me." I bring my lips close to her ear, trying not to raise my voice.

"They are not looking at you, they are looking at me. They call me 'the Widow on the Motorcycle.'" She shouts back to me as she accelerates the motorcycle and bypasses the donkey and the cart. Still, not wanting to see their looks around me, I lower my head towards her back and close my eyes while holding on to her.

"We are here." I hear her voice and open my eyes.

The motorcycle is in the village square. Around us are several buildings and shops. In the center of the square I see the ruined fountain that Francesca once told me about. Several women huddle around the fountain, holding their water cans,and filling them from the tap. They scold the smiling children running around them, playing on the cobblestones. Near them, I see a single older man in a suit walking slowly, lost in thought.

"Did you bring me to your village to show me what we have destroyed?" I look around and see the abandoned building that must have once been a movie theater, the sky is now noticeably visible through its walls. A movie poster featuring a beautiful actress with a seductive look in her eyes still decorates one of the building's walls. Below it are torn posters glorifying Mussolini ,covered with red paint.

"Come with me." Francesca hands me the crutches ignoring my question. She walks down the square, cursing the children running towards the motorcycle shouting, "La vedova en moto, La vedova en moto."

Follow her and keep on looking down, beware not to slip on the pavement, ignore the looks of the women who turn around and stare and the children who run after us and shout, amputato, amputato.

They're calling her names, not me. Where is she taking me? Does she want to leave me here alone in the square? Is she trying to teach me a lesson? I follow her as fast as I can, occasionally looking up, noticing her black dress against the white backdrop of the village square.

"Come this way." She enters one of the shops at the end of the square and says something to the older man who stands in the doorway. He answers something back and looks at me for a moment. Where did she bring me to?

The interior of the small workshop is dim and cool. All around there are carpentry' tools and small furniture. It smells of sawdust and varnish. Why am I here?

Francesca starts talking to the shop

owner pointing at my leg. I can hear him talking, repeating the word 'Americana' and shaking his head. Francesca raises her voice in return. Meanwhile, I stand there looking at them not understanding a word they are saying.

"Wait here." She tells me before leaving the workshop, disappearing outside. I find myself all alone with the older Italian man. He stands there playing with his mustache, looking at me and smiling.

"Americana?"

"Si."

He comes closer and offers me a chair. I sit down and watch him as he goes back to his desk drawer. He takes out a measuring tape, approaches me, and kneels down by my leg. He raises his head to look at me:

"Si?" He asks.

"Si," I answer but I do not understand what he means nor what he wants from me.

Slowly and gently, he rolls up my hospital pants, exposing my amputated leg, examining it closely.

"Si?"

"Si."

His fingers loosen the bandages around my leg, gently removing them, and I close my eyes. I don't want to see the look on his face when he sees my ugly leg stump. My fingers grip the arms of the chair tightly as I feel his rough fingers gently touching my stump.

"Si?" I open my eyes and see him smiling at me from the floor, his hand touching my one single shoe.

"Si," I answer him, and he removes my shoe and sock, placing my bare foot on the wooden floor.

After examining the leg that remained and the one that I lost, he measures both of them, pulls out a pencil behind his ear, and begins to write numbers on a piece of paper that he had laid out on the floor.

A noise coming from the entrance makes me raise my head, and I see Francesca entering the workshop, followed by another older man wearing a gray robe.

The two men start talking or perhaps arguing, but I do not understand a thing. The man wearing the robe pulls out several strips of leather from his pocket and approaches my leg. He places the leather on my stump, and the two men proceed arguing. All I can understand is "Si" and "Americana." Finally they seem to agree on something. They finish their examination of my leg, sum up their lists, and rise from the floor. I can see them smiling at me, saying something in Italian.

"Stand up," Francesca tells me.

I hold on to the back of the chair and stand up. To my surprise, I can see the faces of some children who now stand outside the workshop, curiously peeking inside through the filthy window. They are smiling at me.

The two men bend at my feet again

and continue to measure as I stand in the center of the small room, supporting myself with my crutches. I look down at their hands; they are drawing sketches on the pieces of paper lying on the floor in front of them. Still, my thoughts remain focused on the children and their questioning eyes outside.

"They are not looking at you, they are looking at me," Francesca tells me when she notices the direction I'm looking at, but I tend not to believe her.

"Andarsene, go away" She walks out of the store for a moment and yells at them. I can hear them running away laughing, but not a moment passes until I can see their faces in the window again. Now I have no choice but to smile at them awkwardly, and I can see them smiling back at me, waving their hands.

"Cigarettes, do you have any cigarettes?" Francesca asks me when the two men stand up again, smiling at me and arguing with her. I pull out my box of cigarettes and hand it over to her. She then divides them equally between the two men as they shake her hand. The shoemaker nods towards me, leaving the workshop as we say goodbye to him as well as the carpenter.

"Get yourself some boxes of cigarettes, so we have something to pay them later." She tells me when we get back to the motorcycle, banishing away the swarm of children following us.

"Thank you," I whisper to her, my

lips close to her ear, as we begin our ride back. I hug her tightly, but she does not answer me. Maybe she did not 'hear me.

"Where have you been?" Audrey yells at us from the hospital entrance when Francesca stops the motorcycle and turns to help me with my crutches.

"I felt ill. I asked the Italian to take me for a ride for some air." I shout back at her.

"Hurry up, there is still cleaning to do," she says to Francesca and disappears back into the hospital. I look at Fracescs who is waiting for me, to help me off the motorcycle.

"How long have you had this motorcycle for?" I ask her.

"It was my husband's motorcycle." She answers and strokes the handlebars for a moment. "He taught me how drive it the summer before the war began. Before the fascists forced him to enlist in the army and sent him to Russia to fight with the Nazis." She spits on the ground as she utters the words 'Fascists' and 'Nazis' and turns her back to me. Marching in her airy black dress, she enters the hospital white building, and heads to clean the nurses' room.

***

"Wake up." I feel a hand touching me. A few days have passed since our visit to the village. I open my eyes and see Francesca again.

"Are we going to the village?"

"Si." She nods at me.

"One moment." I sit in my bed, bending over and taking out my army duffel bag from the locker. I pull the bag onto the bed and empty all of its contents and hide them underneath my blanket.

"John," I whisper to him and touch his shoulder. I do not like to wake him up, but I need something from him right now.

"What, Grace?" He turns to me, and I suspect he's been awake for a little while now.

"Can I borrow your army duffle bag?"

"Yes." He answers me, turning around with his back to me again.

"Don't you want to ask why?"

"No."

"It's for a good cause."

"I'm sure it is." He replies, with his back still turned towards me.

For a moment, I want to hug him to cheer him up, but I know it's not my job. There is another nurse who takes care of him.

"I'll be back soon." I touch his shoulder and pull his duffel bag out of the locker. I empty his personal belongings and hand the bag to Francesca, who had been standing there watching us this whole time. "Let's go."

On the ground floor, instead of going out to the front driveway, I lead her to the kitchen supply cabin.

“Good Morning.” I stand in front of the sergeant in charge of the kitchen.

“The Commanding Nurse had asked you to give me some food cans.”

“And why does the Commanding Nurse need these food cans?” He answers, his tone slightly dismissive.

“Because she wants to have a surprise picnic for the nurses who have been working so hard.”

“And do you have a request note from her stating that?” He approaches, looking down at me.

“No. Do you really want me to have to hobble back on my crutches and get you a request note?” I raise my eyes and look up at him, hoping he will not send me back out of there.

"And who is this? Is she having a picnic too?" He looks at Francesca.

"Do you think I'm able to carry anything? That is why I brought the Italian along."

He thinks for a moment before entering the kitchen's supply cabinet, and yelled: "What do you need?"

"Canned meat, dried milk, orange juice powder, tea, coffee, and chocolate," I yell back.

This time, Francesca drives the loaded motorcycle much slower, careful not to roll over the potholes. "La vedova en moto!" The smiling children playing on the remains of the tanks decorating the entrance to the village shout to us. But Francesca doesn't answer them. The women on the street stare at us, and the square at the center of the village looks exactly the same as the last time, with the destroyed fountain and the movie theater where all you can see now is a glimpse of the morning sky shining through its ceiling.

"Bonjourno." The carpenter smiles at me as we enter. He hurries out behind his wooden desk, hands me a chair, and gestures me to sit down.

Then he bends down and takes out a wooden leg from behind the counter. My wooden leg.

***

It is made of light wood covered with varnish and has leather straps at the top of it. The straps are there so I can tie it to my stump. The wooden leg has a metal joint at the ankle area that allows for the movement of the foot.

Francesca disappears again and returns after a minute with the shoemaker by her side. As I look up, I can barely see the children' waving at me behind the filthy window through the tears in my eyes.

"Si?" The carpenter asks me as he leans by my foot.

"Si." I nod at him and wipe the tears away as he gently rolls up the ugly hospital pants and removes the bandages. He presses the wooden leg against the stump, examining the fit.

The wood is cold and smooth and hard against my skin, and I can feel a little pain. He turns around, says something to Francesca, and they start arguing. Again I do not understand a thing, but suddenly Francesca takes off her shoes and socks and hands the socks to him. The old carpenter takes one of the socks and puts it on my stump. Then he does the same thing with the other sock and examines the fit of the wooden leg once more. He says something to Francesca and she yells in Italian to the kids outside; I can hear them laughing, and after a few seconds, more socks are thrown from into the workshop.

The carpenter puts them all on my stump, one on top of the other, then he places the wooden leg against the socks, ties it with the leather straps, stands up and smiles at me.

"Si." He gestures me to stand up. I hold his hands, and for the first time since that horrible day, I manage to stand up without the crutches. I'm still unstable, and still shaking while holding on to the carpenter's hands. But I'm standing up without my hated crutches.

Slowly, I manage to walk through the small room, holding on to the carpenter's hands. I look down and see the prosthetic leg pressed against my stump. Despite the socks trying to soften the wood, I can still feel the pressure. After a few steps, I feel myself needing to rest. It will take me time to get used to the new leg. But right now I'm trying to get used to the smiling children at the window and the two older men patting my shoulder, saying "bravo, bravo." I drag the two bags full of food cans and chocolates and hand them over together with the cigarette boxes. Suddenly, I look at Francesca standing near the shop's entrance and realize how inconsiderate I must seem. I take some food cans and cigarette boxes from the pile, get up, and give them to her. She refuses at first, but I insist, joined by the carpenter and the shoemaker, who also urge her to take them. She finally agrees and lets me fill her hands. The carpenter goes to the back of the counter, takes out a bottle of wine and passes it around. Everyone laughs as I bring the bottle to my lips and sip from it.

Still using my crutches, I walk slowly back to the motorcycle; the carpenter, the showmaker, and the children all follow me, walking by my side. Even some of the women pumping water in the village square, stop and join them. I can already feel myself stepping on the new foot as I walk.

"Grazie, grazie" I keep thanking them. It seems to me that maybe Francesca and I drank a little bit too much of that wine, but it's hard for me to tell for sure. Every few steps, I pause and bend over to stroke my new wooden leg, while everybody smiles and cheers.

On our way back to the hospital, I seem to remember Francesca and I singing. I hug her tightly as the motorcycle changes its speed, depending on the song we sing. I do not really know what the songs are about as they are all in Italian. Maybe these are not songs at all, maybe she's trying to tell me a story. It does not really matter to me. The trees pass by us so fast, and I just want to spread my hands and fly, but I must hold on to her not to fall off the motorcycle. I notice a pleasant aroma of wine wafting from her.

It's almost sunset when we get back to the hospital. Francesca helps me climb up the stairs at the hospital's entrance, which now seem really high to me. I think I remember asking Audrey to help me go up the stairs as well, but she refuses.

"Good night, John." I whisper to him as I lie back in my bed, nauseous. "I have been fixed." But he does not answer me, maybe he is already asleep.

***

9. To Dance.

"Dear John, the autumn winds are already starting to blow," I lie in bed late at night and read John a new letter from Georgia. He turns his back to me and doesn't respond. I don't even know whether he is listening to me or not.

"John, can you hear me? A new letter has arrived," I say to him again. I spent the whole afternoon sitting behind the warehouse writing to John, looking for the right words of encouragement. It's better than telling him she has left him for another.

"What is she writing? Is she missing me?" He finally answers. At least he's not sleeping.

"Yes. She writes that she's waiting to hug you and walk hand in hand through the main street of your town."

"So maybe you should tell her that blind people don't walk hand in hand. It seems to me that she doesn't know it yet." Then he turns to face me, "on the other hand, you already know how to lead me. Maybe we will write to her that she should find someone else, and you will stay here with me and continue leading me? You already know how to do it well. Unless another German airplane suddenly emerges out of the black sky...for me the sky is black even when the sun is shining."

"John, she's waiting for you."
I hold the letter, looking at my handwriting. What else can I do

to encourage him? Would it help if I wrote him more letters in her name?

"She's not waiting for me. She's waiting for another John to sit next to her by the fireplace and read her books. Do you think I can read books?"

"She will read books to you."

"Yes, just like you protected me when the German airplane arrived." His voice is so loud that it could wake up the other wounded sleeping in the hall.

"It's not the same."

"Really?" He sits up in bed and extends his hand in my direction, "Hand me the letter so I can practice reading."

"No, John, I'm not giving you the letter."

"It's mine, isn't it?" He motions his hand in the air, extends it forward, approaching me, touching my chest, stroking my breast for a second. I want to get away from him and his outstretched hand, but I'm afraid of falling out of bed.

"I apologize," he pulls his hand back and backs away in his bed, but the feeling of his warm fingers remains on my body.

"Take it." I crumple the letter and toss it at him, and in the dark, it seems to me that it hits his face.

"I'm sorry, I didn't know I would touch you. I didn't know you were so close."

"It's okay." I stroke the spot where

his hand had just touched me, surprised by the feeling spreading through my body.

"No, it's not okay. A man should not behave like that. I apologize."

"John, it's okay," I want to get close to him and take the letter back, but I know it's not possible now. I shouldn't have thrown it in his face. "You couldn't see me."

"That's exactly the point. I'm blind."

"It's not the point. The point is that there is a woman who loves you and is waiting for you at home." I imagine his hand stroking Georgia.

"Tell me, Grace, when is your ship coming? Aren't you supposed to recover already and stop feeling sorry for me?"

"Is everything okay here?" I hear Audrey's voice. How long has she been standing there listening to us? Did she see what had happened?

"Yeah, everything's fine," John answers her.

"Because I heard noises coming from your direction." I see her placing a hand on his shoulder in the dark.

"I was just trying to get off the bed, and I accidentally bumped into the locker and woke Grace up." He answers her.

"So, she lit a candle on top of the locker?"

"She just wanted to see what happened. She's not blind like me."

"Grace, you can go back to sleep,"

she turns to me, "I will take care of him." It seems that she is smiling at me in the dark. I turn my back towards them and can hear her whispering something to him; he whispers something back.

I look at the wall, trying to count the lines I had drawn, but Audrey blows the candle out, and I can no longer see anything with the dim light coming from the nurses' station. It's going to happen soon, I know it.

Maybe a German submarine will hit the ship? Not hard enough to make it sink, but maybe only to cause some small damage that would delay its arrival? No wonder she thinks I love the Germans. I keep hearing them talking quietly in the dark, trying not to listen to what John is saying to her. Still, my body remembers the feeling of his hand on my breast.

***

"Americana, Americana." I feel a hand shaking my body a few nights later. What do they want from me?

"Americana, wake up." The voice calls again. I open my eyes in the dark and gather that it's Francesca. Her face is close to mine, and she's whispering to me.

"What?" I answer her. The hall is dark and quiet, what time is it?

"The ship." She whispers to me.

"What about the ship?"

"It has arrived at the port. A

telegram arrived." She keeps shaking me, "Wake up. I heard the nurses talking."

I sit up in bed and look at her. She is standing close to me, and I can notice her dark silhouette. What should I do?

"You have to run away. You're on the list." She keeps whispering to me, "I heard them talking about you," and I look at her for a moment and say nothing. I ran away once. They will not let me run away again. My time has come.

"Thanks," I whisper to her and lie back in my bed, looking in John's direction. At least he didn't wake up.

"Americana, wake up. You have to do something." She shakes me again, but I keep lying in my bed.

I wanted to return to be a nurse again so badly, but they won't let me, not in this place. Nothing can change their mind. My new wooden leg will accompany me on my way home.

"Americana, aren't you doing something?"

"There's nothing I can do." I have been trying to think of an idea for days without much success.

"You have to do something."

"Sorry," I answer to her in the dark, "it's time for me to go home."

"For an Americana who doesn't understand anything, you really don't understand anything."

"Sorry, you have a village to return to, and I have a ship waiting for me. I can't run away again; they wouldn't let me."

"And I thought you were my friend." She says, muttering something in Italian that sounds like a curse. I want to explain that I have no choice, but then I see her dark silhouette disappear behind the curtain, leaving me in the quiet hall with silent John and the black night.

Time passes as I lie in bed, watching the dark ceiling and the curtain that separates John and me from the rest of the wounded. What would John tell me to do? Would he advise me to try and do something? Escape again? For a moment, I want to wake him up and ask him for his opinion. But ever since he had touched me that night, we have hardly spoken. Every morning, I rush to get dressed and walk away from, and he doesn't try to get close to me either. At least I found the letter I had written in Georgia's name on the floor. It was torn and I taped it back together, even though I should have burned it. But it doesn't matter now, the ship is waiting for me, and I am on the list. A nurse will come in and read my name in a few hours. No one can save me from being shipped back home.

"May I help you?" The nurse on duty looks up from the book she is reading and stares at me. I don't know her. She has never taken care of me. What do I tell her?

"The list, where is it?"

She hands me the sheet of paper, and I look at the names written on it. Francesca wasn't wrong. I'm on the list.

"I'm sorry. I heard what happened last time." She tells me. She probably already heard the story about the nurse who lost her leg and wanted to stay but must go home tomorrow.

"Do you have a typewriter?" I ask her.

"What do you need it for?"

"I need a typewriter. Will you let me sit here for a few minutes?"

She smiles at me and gets up, takes a typewriter out of one of the closets and places it on the table. "Help yourself."

"What are you doing?" She asks as I shove the smooth paper in the paper guide and turn the knob, placing the list on the table next to me. What should I answer her?

"I am writing a letter."

"I can't let you do that." She looks at me, and I remove my hand from the keys, thinking the only idea I had just failed.

"Grace?" She tells me a moment later and gets up from the small table.

"Yes?"

"I can't let you do that, but I have

to go out for a few minutes to check on the wounded. Can you please stay at the station and make sure everything is fine?" And she walks out the door and disappears into the dark, not waiting for me to answer.

My fingers type the list of names on the paper as fast as possible, hoping that the keystrokes do not wake anyone. I need to hurry, but I'm careful not to make typing mistakes. I never liked the typing lessons we had in high school; they were meant to prepare us for being helpful secretaries.

"A good secretary that types without mistakes is a crucial part of her boss's success." Mrs. Friesman lectured us as she walked through the classroom, holding a wooden stick in her hand, and hitting the fingers of those who typed wrong. "Grace, you would make a very bad secretary," she would say and hit my fingers.

"Grace, do you need help?" I hear the nurse a few minutes later.

"Read me the names," I whisper to her and type as fast as I can, making sure not to mix up the identification numbers of the soldiers going home tomorrow.

From the window, I can see the sun beginning to rise as I lay cowering in my bed, waiting for the nurse to enter the hall and start reading from the list. My fingers keep on peeling the plaster off the wall.

"Adam." I hear the nurse voice and cower further in my bed.

"Going home."

"Arlo." She keeps reading.

"Grace, are you okay?" John whispers to me. I turn to him and place my hand on his fingers feeling their warmth on the white bed.

"Billy." The nurse keeps reading names off the list, and I feel John's fingers grip mine. I close my eyes and feel myself holding on tighter with each name being called off.

"Grace, I think she's done reading the list." I hear John's voice and open my eyes. I see the soldiers standing by their beds, saying goodbye to their friends, preparing for the voyage home, but I continue to hold his fingers tightly. I earned another month, but next time it will not be enough. If I want to be a nurse again, I must do more.

***

"Can you move fast?"

"No, Head Nurse Blanche." I'm standing in her office. I walked in a few minutes ago without knocking on the door. I want her to hear what I have to say.

"Can you run?"

"I helped the wounded when the planes attacked us." She would not let me into her office anyway. Her door is always closed.

"Yes, you definitely helped." She looks at me, touching and arranging her gray hair, even though it's already perfectly pulled back as if prepared for an army muster. "I have no idea how you did it without your feet. Lucky you weren't injured either."

"I want to be a nurse again." I hold my head high, repeating what I said when I had burst in two minutes ago. Before that, I stood outside her office for a long time, whispering to myself the very same words I would say to her. But now I have forgotten everything I wanted to say, and I'm repeating myself saying that I want to be a nurse again over and over.

"I'm sorry, but how exactly do you want to be a nurse when you were only an intern before, and now you can barely even walk?"

"I have a new leg." I take a step back and pull my pants up, exposing my prosthetic. I have been struggling with the leather strips all morning long and the wooden leg hurts me after a few minutes of walking, but she can't know that. I smile at her pleasantly as if it doesn't hurt at all, trying not to lean on my crutches, even though I brought them with me.

"Very impressive." She doesn't look at my prosthetic leg. "How did you manage to organize that?" She keeps reading from the paper lying in front of her on the table, the same one she was reading when I burst into her office.

"I had some help." I don't want to tell her about Francesca, but it doesn't seem that she cares about my leg either way.

"Yes, I heard that someone had organized a party for the nurses, supplied by U.S. Army food." She writes something on a piece of paper and without looking up at me, "I don't understand at all how you are still here. You were supposed to be on the ship on your way to Gibraltar, continuing to New York harbor from there." She finally raises her eyes from the paper and examines me as if looking for further information on my face.

"They didn't read my name." I look back at her. She mustn't suspect I had anything to do with it.

My leg starts hurting again, and I move a little, trying to get used to my new shoe. I have no idea where one of the nurses found me another shoe. For months now, I have been walking around with only one shoe. I had lost the other one somewhere, maybe during that day, amongst the burning and the screaming.

"So, when you are ready to walk, run, and carry the wounded, you can come again here and reapply to be a nurse. Until then, I will make sure you are on the list of the next ship leaving here." She lowers her gaze and looks back at the paper lying in front of her.

For a moment, I want to scream at her to look at me and see how hard I am trying, but I don't think she really cares. She is interested only in the papers on her desk and her tidy hospital.

"Thank you, Head Nurse Blanche." I turn and intend to leave. I will learn to walk and run and carry the wounded, and I will ask her again. I will not give up anymore.

"You're welcome, have a nice day."

"At least she didn't ask me to dance," I whisper to myself as I push on the door handle.

"Dancing is good too." I hear her mumble before I close the door behind me.

***

"Go ahead, Americana, catch me." Francesca walks away from me on the main road, holding my crutches in her hands.

"Stay where you are, La vedova en moto," I shout to her while walking slowly, keeping my eyes on the road in order not to fall but also to avoid the staring glances of the people standing at the entrance to the hospital.

"Americana, your wooden sticks are waiting for you." She lifts my crutches in the air and keeps moving away from me, making sure that I don't catch her. She's completely crazy if she thinks I can walk all that way. I can't walk more than a few steps in a row.

Despite the socks I wrap over my stump, it still hurts me. But I don't intend to give up. Step by step, I walk on the empty road. I will show them that I am not disabled.

"Americana, you are not allowed to rest." She calls me when I stop for a second and rearrange the socks over my leg. These are not the socks I received from the village children. I keep those as a souvenir, even though I know I must return them. They probably need them more than I do.

"You are very slow, Americana." I stand and look at her from time to time, but most of the time, I look down, trying to keep myself stable, swinging my prosthetic after my healthy leg, trying to move forward.

"Another step," I whisper to myself, ignoring the pain. Despite the pleasant afternoon sun, I'm sweating as if we are in the middle of the summer and not in early fall. "Another step." I'm looking at the road, careful not to slip. "Another step," and I finally reach Francesca.

"Come on, Italiana, you can't keep running away from me." I smile through the sweat and the pain. She stands still as I look up and see them.

From a distance, they look like a gray mass surrounded by a cloud of dust rising from the ground. They approach us in long, endless lines, walking on the main road, and I can hear their army boots hitting the broken asphalt.

"Let's move," I whisper to Francesca, but she stays standing in the middle of the road, watching them.

They wear gray uniforms, stained with mud and dust. They walk in two straight rows, followed by a few American soldiers aiming their guns at them, making sure they don't try to escape. They march and approach us, passing us by without stopping even for a second. Most of them have curly light hair and an indifferent look on their face. Some still have rank marks of the German army on their shoulders.

"Vorrei che tu morissi." Francesca says to a German officer. She approaches him, spitting in his face as he continues to march, looking straight ahead.

"Vorrei che tu morissi, I wish you would die." She approaches the next soldier, spitting at him as well.

"Vorrei che tu morissi, I wish you would die." She tries to push the next soldier as he moves away from her, looking forward and marching ahead.

"Vorrei che tu morissi. Bring my husband back!" She screams at the German soldiers, grabs my crutches, and attacks them, beginning to hit and spit at a German POW carrying an officers' rank. "Bring my husband back."

"Francesca," I scream at her as an American soldier from the guard runs up to her, holds and pulls her away from the center of the road. She tries to hit him and free herself, spitting at the German soldiers passing them by.

"Francesca," I shout at her again and walk carefully in her direction, lowering my eyes not wanting to see the Germans. They move out of the way for me, stopping for just a moment before they pass me by. I can smell their sour sweat and hear their labored breathing. I keep walking through the rows of soldiers, coughing and trying to reach her. I forcibly grab her hand and she clings onto me, while the American soldier drags both of us to the side of the road, finally releasing her.

"Bring my husband back." She breaks down crying on the side of the road while I bend down by her side, hugging her shoulders covered with wild black hair. We both sit on the side of the road, her black dress dirty with dust and tears. "Bring my husband back." She doesn't stop crying, as the column of German prisoners passes us by. Their light hair covered with dust, their eyes looking forward while their boots hit the ground at a steady pace as if they were thunderous drums.

"Let's get out of here," I whisper to her as the last of the German prisoners walks by, followed by two American soldiers armed with rifles. One of them stands for a moment and salutes us, even though I am not an officer and Francesca is an Italian.

"Let's get out of here," I whisper to her again, and we both get up. Holding each other, we walk slowly down the deserted road, picking up my crutches from the asphalt.

***

"Did you meet him before the war broke out?" I ask her after a few minutes. She looks back at the empty road, walks a few steps to the side, and sits down resting on a stone fence.

"You Americans think that wars start in one day, just as the Japanese attacked you in Pearl Harbor. You must think that wars have a start date and an end date," she replies after a few seconds. "But you understand nothing. Wars don't start with bombs and airplanes and explosions; wars start with silence." She holds out her hand, and I take the box of cigarettes out of my shirt pocket and hand her one.

"I was only a girl when my father went out one evening to demonstrate against the fascists." She lights the cigarette and starts talking, "He came back at night with his whole suit stained with blood." Her hands tremble as she holds her cigarette, inhaling the smoke. "My big, strong father who would pick me up on his shoulders and laugh out loud, could barely walk that night, his shirt was so bloody red." She stops talking for a moment, "Mussolini's bullies, the people in the black shirts." She says contemptuously, "would walk the streets, beating all those who dared to go out and demonstrate or strike." She pauses before continuing her story.

"Mother wanted to take him to hospital." She slowly exhales the smoke towards the setting sun. "But he refused. He said they would probably look for him there and arrest him. He recovered, but he never went back to how he was before that, my big, strong father."

"You know?" She turns to me. "The war started many years before the newspapers wrote about it starting."

I think of my home in Chicago, and my dad, who had never demonstrated against anything in his life, and lower my eyes.

"Then, they started to control and

monitor us. In every way possible." She continues.

"If you wanted to study, you had to be a member of the fascist youth movement, and if you wanted to be a factory manager, you had to be a member of the fascist party, and if you wanted to contact a government official about a particular problem and actually have anyone listen to you, you had to be a fascist party member." She keeps on talking, "anything that you wanted to do, you had to be one of them. You had to bow down to Mussolini, the Duce. And you had to choose, to bow down, or live in fear."

"Fear of what?" I ask, lighting a cigarette for myself.

"Fear of the nights." She goes on

pausing for a moment, "in fear that someone will report you and then they will come at night to arrest you. They always came at night. They loved the night. It wasn't for nothing that they called themselves the black shirts and chose black uniforms." She spits on the dirt road. "For years, I lived in fear of the night. I hate the night. But that's how I met him too."

"Your husband?"

"Yes, my husband."

"At night?"

"Do you know how it is that you are young and stupid and believe that you will be able to change the world?" She looks at me.

"Yes," I answer her, remembering how I would run out of our house window and go out to meet my girlfriends. We would go to stand outside the dance halls in the center of town, watching the women dance, feeling so bold and free. Now, compared to Francesca, it feels so childish.

"It was before the 'real' war, before they started reporting on it in the newspapers." She speaks slowly, "we were a group of young people who believed we would be able to stop them, so we decided to rebel, like young people do. How naïve we must have been." She smiles to herself. "So we went to Rome, where no one could recognize us."

"And what happened?"

"We wrote a graffiti against Mussolini on some wall of a building. We didn't have the courage to do anything more than that. But we heard footsteps and feared it was the police or the black shirts and fled."

"And it was then when you met him?"

"They all disappeared. My friends and I, we all ran in different directions, and I walked alone for hours on the streets, imagining that I was going to be caught. It was already evening, and of course, I was late for the last bus back home." She points her head towards her village. "I was just standing between the platforms of the empty bus station, panting and worried I would meet a bunch of black shirt bullies, when he showed up with his motorcycle and took me back to the village." I notice her smiling to herself. "I asked him to take me. I had to ask someone, and it turned out I asked someone who would want to buy me a dress a year later."

"He sure is a lovely man."

"He said we would not be able to stop Mussolini's fascists, and I said we would succeed, and he was right." She puts out her hand, and I take the box of cigarettes out of my pocket and hand her another one.

"And he wanted to buy me a dress with flowers on it. I didn't agree because I told him it's bad luck when a man buys a dress for a woman. He didn't buy me the dress, but I was wrong; in the end, I was left without a floral dress and with bad luck."

"You couldn't possibly know." I

exhale my cigarette smoke into the air, watching the sky getting darker.

"He hated the fascists even more than I did, but he had no choice. He had to draft into the army, otherwise, he would be hanged for treason. You see, we couldn't choose which side to be on."

I want to tell her something encouraging, but I can't think of anything as I wipe the tears from my eyes.

"So, he wasn't killed by the fascists. Instead, he disappeared in Russia and must have been killed by the Red Army." She looks at me, and I can see that she's crying too.

"You don't know it. Maybe he was taken as a prisoner of war and is still alive."

"Yes, you never know," she looks at the empty road where the German prisoners of war had just passed. "The dress was so beautiful, and I wanted it so badly, but we just got married, and it cost so much, and I thought we should not waste so much money. You never know what the future holds. I hate Rome."

"You never know what the future holds." I lightly hit the stone terrace with my wooden foot.

"At least I have someone to smoke with."

"The lame with the wooden leg and the widow with the motorcycle." I smile at her when we get up, and she supports me as we walk back towards the hospital.

"Let's go around," I ask her, looking

at the hospital entrance, as we enter through the destroyed iron gate. Near the wide steps of the entrance to the building, where once the landlord and his wife must have stood wearing their formal evening clothes, greeting the guests who arrived in their Rolls-Royce and Bentley cars, now stands a military jeep marked with the white American star. Instead of lavish dinner guests, nurses are now sitting on the steps, talking to the two pilots standing in front of them.

"Is everything alright?" She asks me as I turn towards the stone wall, looking for the gap in the wall that allows us to go through to the garden and the back entrance of the hospital.

"I just want to see the sunset," I tell her, but even though she doesn't answer, I think she doesn't believe me. One of the nurses laughs out loud and stands up in front of the pilots, swaying and making dance movements. I used to love dancing so much once.

***

"1944, the victory will happen this year." Back then, in the ballroom in Chicago, the sentence was clearly written on the poster that hung from the ceiling, spread wide from one side of to the other. This was less than a year ago, right before I boarded the train that would take me to New York harbor and then to the war.

"1944, look up." The announcer

at the New Year's ball in Chicago shouted to the crowd, and a huge cloud of balloons fell from the ceiling to the sounds of our excited cheers.

"Look," I called happily and pointed to the red and white balloons that had fallen on our heads, ignoring the sweat pouring from me after hours of dancing. I think his name was Fred, the soldier who danced with me all through that evening. He was wearing a white navy uniform, and he hadn't yet received any war medals. He tried to kiss me, explaining that he was headed to San Francisco on his way to Hawaii the very next day. He promised to beat the Japanese and come back to Chicago to marry me.

"You don't know me at all." I laughed at him, raising my voice to overcome the loud music, as I held on to his broad shoulders, adjusted my steps to his, and let him put a hand on my waist. My eyes were looking around at all the soldiers dancing with their girls, maybe for the last time just like for Fred and me.

"I'll kill the Japs so fast that I'd be back before you have time to forget me." He brought his lips to my ears, hoping I would kiss him.

"I'm going tomorrow too," I said to him, and it seemed to me that he didn't hear me at all, but I didn't care. All I cared about was dancing with a handsome soldier that held me in his arms, with all the other soldiers and beautiful women surrounding us.

"Where are you going?"

"To the war." I laughed and let him hold me tighter, knowing that I would board the train to New York the next day to begin a new and exciting adventure.

He left me alone on the dancing floor for a few moments and then returned, holding two glasses of champagne. "To the war, for bringing people together."

"To the war and to all the adventures ahead of us." I smiled at him and sipped the sweet drink. And as we kept on dancing, he slightly lowered his hand resting on my back, and I didn't move it away. Still, I did not let him kiss me, even when the evening was over, and we said goodbye at the entrance to the ballroom. I promised to meet again, knowing it would never happen. I think I didn't even tell him my name, knowing that he would look for another girl to dance with in San Francisco or Hawaii the next day or the next week. I was okay with that. I knew that I would have many more chances to dance.

At the end of that evening, my legs hurt, and the high heels bothered me so much that I wanted to remove them and walk home barefoot. It was almost dawn, and I had to hurry and pack for the train, but I walked home slowly, smiling at the paperboys. That night, the war was so exciting.

But now, the hall of the wounded is quiet at night, and I'm reading a book to John, not knowing if he's listening to me or already asleep.

He lies in bed all day and refuses to go out to the garden. He also refuses to let me read Georgia's old letters. I'm afraid to tell him that she had left him. I'm also afraid to write him another letter that could somehow reveal that I'm lying, too. I close the book and look at him. I must stop thinking about that. He's not my problem. He has Audrey, who strokes his hair every morning and takes care of him, smiling at him constantly.

"John, do you like to dance?"

"I'm blind, Grace, blind people don't dance." He whispers towards the ceiling.

"John, I need your help," I whisper back to him.

"Are you offering me a walk in

the garden? Actually, it could be nice." He says quietly while I approach him, "Maybe we could invite some German airplanes to attack us again. Then I could lie in the dark and wonder if this time the airplanes would finish what the previous ones had failed to do. I might try and think about where I could run and hide, but it doesn't matter either way." He keeps on talking. "Because either way, I can't run away from them even if I tried. I'm blind."

"John, enough with that. They were here and now they are gone. You survived, isn't that the important part?"

"Grace, have you ever felt helpless?" He reaches out into the air but doesn't move towards me, perhaps afraid of touching me again, like he did last time.

"John, we were all wounded by this war." I'm getting closer to him, placing my hand on his arm.

"No, Grace, not all of us are like those wounded who are in pain right now but will recover, keeping only the memories of their injury," he holds me too, and I feel the warmth of his fingers. "I mean, have you ever felt really helpless; that it doesn't matter what you do, it's not up to you anymore?"

"Yeah, John, I have felt like that. I have been feeling that way for months." I release his hand from my shoulder. He doesn't really listen to me, no matter what I say.

"Then you probably understand me." He leans back and looks up at the ceiling. What should I tell him?

I watch him lie motionless in his bed, as if waiting for me to assure him that he will recover; to assure him that nothing and no one else would attack him. How can I promise him that?

"I understand you," I finally say, "but, out of all of the soldiers and the nurses and walking in the garden that day, you were the first one to recognize the danger, and then you laid down and covered your head. You tried to do the best you could. You weren't helpless, you were never helpless, even now when you're blind." I try to find the right words, I keep looking at him as he looks at the ceiling instead of my direction, but I know I'm failing. "You're blind, and you're alive, and I'm just asking for your help, not because I feel sorry for you, but because I think you're the best person to help me," I whisper to him, trying not to raise my voice so that the nurse on duty doesn't have a reason to come and check on us.

But he doesn't answer, and I lie down in my bed and continue reading the book, wanting to take a pencil, mark and erase all the parts where the hero succeeds at the end.

"Americana, what do you need help with?" He asks after a while. "I heard the Italian woman calling you that name."

"It's dark outside now, so no airplane will be coming to attack us." I feel his hand gripping my shoulders as we walk slowly through the front driveway of the hospital, listening to the sound of gravel under our feet.

"We're standing in the front driveway. There's no one here to look at us." I tell him, looking around at the silhouettes of the military trucks and jeeps parked underneath the cypress trees. "There is a big Red Cross flag spread on the ground," but in the dark, I can't see the bullet holes left by the Germans' attack. If it was less dark, I could probably see the bullet marks on the building wall.

"There are only the two of us here." I stand in front of him.

"And I need you to dance with me." I let the crutches fall on the gravel and hold his hands, placing them on my waist.

I can feel the warmth of his hands through my hospital shirt as he holds me gently. I place my hands on his arms, feeling his shoulder muscles while we both begin to slowly sway from side to side, making sure not to step on each other. The only sound I can hear is the creaking of the gravel underneath our feet, while I try to stabilize my wooden leg, teaching myself to walk again.

What does he think of me? I look up at him, but in the dark, I can only see his silhouette looking towards the trees. I hold myself back from resting my head on his chest.

"Grace, is everything okay?" He asks after a while as we continue to move slowly in the center of the front driveway.

"Yes, everything is fine." I look up and smile at him even though he's unable to see me, not telling him that I'm in pain.

My wooden leg sinks into the gravel with every step, and I feel the pain of my injury. I hold John tightly to reduce the pressure on my stump, and I fight the urge to clench my palms into fists from the pain. It hurts so much, but I won't give up. I can feel tears of pain running down my cheeks; luckily, he can't see.

"Are you sure everything's fine?"

"Yes, I'm missing the music."

"We can hum."

"I'm too shy to be heard. We're so close to the entrance of the hospital."

"So, let's get further away from here, take me somewhere else."

I must hold his hand to pick up the crutches from the ground. We start walking, crossing the iron gate lying at the entrance of the mansion, walking to the main road in front of the hospital.

In the dim light of the moon, I can barely see the road and the trees around us, but there are no vehicles passing here tonight, and we are alone with only the dark trees looking at us.

"It's better here." I hold his waist again and start humming a song by Ella Fitzgerald, moving my feet on the hard asphalt, realizing it hurts me less over here.

It takes him a while to start humming the song along with me.

His hands tighten around my waist, and I get a little closer to him. If someone were to pass by right now, they would think we were a loving couple, But John makes sure to hold himself far enough from me, as I try to adjust to his body movements, being careful not to touch his leg with my wooden leg.

"Are you comfortable?"

"Yes, thank you." I keep leaning on his body, my leg still hurts, but a little less now. I'll have to get used to the pain.

"Do you like this song?" He asks after a while.

"Yes, and you?"

"I'm not used to it."

"You're not used to dancing? I'm

sorry, I did not think about that." I stop dancing and stand, still holding his waist. "I apologize." I look around, searching for my crutches.

"I love to dance," he answers me quietly, "and I enjoy dancing with you," he pauses for a moment. "But I'm not used to dancing with another girl other than Georgia."

"I'm sorry, I didn't think of that."

"She's my girl," he stops holding me and takes a few steps back, leaving me to stand alone in the middle of the dark road. "We used to do everything together since we became a couple in high school. I had never danced with anyone else other than Georgia." He bends down, fumbles with his hands on the asphalt, and sits on the road. "I know I have to write and tell her about my injury and about what had happened to me. I've known this for days now."

"Oh, John." I approach him slowly, careful not to fall.

"Don't pity me." He looks up, "Just don't that, please. You told me before you didn't feel sorry for me."

"I don't." I stop where I am.

"Everyone feels sorry for me, especially the nurses. Audrey caresses my head as if I were a little boy, speaking to me in a motherly tone all day. As if one more caress would improve my blindness."

"I don't." I retract my hand, which was inches away from touching his dark hair.

"Please, at least you of all people, don't feel sorry for me." He keeps on talking while sitting on the empty road, "I know I need to write to her and tell her I'm coming home soon, but not as the John she is hoping to see. I'm a damaged man who can't do anything; I can't work, I can't walk alone in the street not knowing whether to turn right or left." His voice breaks, he starts crying, and even though I'm not supposed to, I take two steps towards him, manage to lean over without falling, and hug him.

"You're not damaged. There isn't a single flaw in you. You'll be okay, you'll see."

"How do you know?" His crying intensifies. "What will I write to her?"

"I don't know," I hug him tightly and whisper into his ear, "but you'll be okay." I feel his entire body trembling. "And as for Georgia, don't tell her you were injured, not yet. You don't have to tell her right now. You can wait on that."

"What does it matter if I wait or not? Do you think it would change her pain when she reads my letter?"

"I don't know what it would change for her," I stroke the back of his neck, "but maybe it would change your pain."

"You don't know a lot of things."

"Yeah, I don't know a lot of things." I keep hugging him, and his warm hands wrap around my body as if trying to hold on to me.

"Let's get away from here, let's go back to the hospital, to our corner," I whisper to him after a few minutes of silence, grabbing him and trying to get up off the road. My leg hurts, and I want to remove the prosthetic. I'm probably only hurting him with my words, either way.

"Can I invite you to dance?" He gets up and reaches out his hands, searches for me, and I guide his hands to hold my waist again.

While we continue to dance in the middle of the empty, dark road, he quietly sings a song by Frank Sinatra. I look up at his tender lips and ignore the pain in my legs. My head rests on his chest even though I know he's not mine.

In the distance, I can see the faint lights of a vehicle approaching. I can hear the engine sound, and we move to the side of the road. A jeep, loaded with cheerful nurses, passing us on a slow drive before turning to the hospital. They get off, laughing, disappearing through the entrance of the building.

"Who were they?" John asks me.

"Audrey and her nurse friends coming back from visiting the pilots."

"They're having fun."

"Yeah, they're having fun." I feel his hands still holding my waist.

"Do you think we can get through this?"

"I'm sure we will," I rest my head on his chest, wanting to keep dancing with him.

10. Herald.

"Doctor, please, don't give up. We can still save him."

Just a few minutes have passed since Audrey approached our corner, telling me that Head Nurse Blanche was asking whether I was still capable of assisting the doctor with the surgery. "Yes," I answered her immediately, leaving the book I have been reading for hours, rushing to attach my wooden leg, and following her. I didn't even try to think why she was being nice to me again or why Blanche remembered me at all. It could be because the operating room nurses went out tonight to meet the pilots, or it could be related to the recent attacks on the German lines in the north and the stream of wounded soldiers that kept on coming.

And now, I'm the only nurse in the operating room, standing in front of the wounded soldier lying on the operating table.

"Save your breath." The doctor shakes his head, "It's a waste of time."

"Please, Doctor," I beg him, knowing that if he dies, Blanche will never give me another chance.

"I can try, but I don't think he will survive." He looks at me, "Are you new here?"

"Yes,"

Audrey agreed to give me a uniform set. I closed the curtain behind me and got dressed as fast as I could.

I was standing with my back turned to John and had to remind myself that it didn't matter, that he couldn't see me either way. And now I'm standing in front of the wounded and trying to look confident. So much time had passed. Why am I the only nurse here? Why is there no one else here to help me?

"Clean and prep him for surgery."

"Right away, Doctor." I smile at him, hold the scissors, and start cutting off his blue-gray uniform, exposing his injured chest. I must not think about him. I must do everything necessary to keep him alive. This is my chance to prove myself.

"I wonder how he got here," I say as the doctor examines the light hairs on his chest while I disinfect his skin with iodine, making sure he is ready.

"I heard two guys brought him here on a jeep." He is holding the scalpel, "They left him at the entrance and hurried back." He examines his wound and starts cutting his skin, "He'd been waiting here for a long time, they couldn't find an available nurse. He might die of blood loss."

"I'm sorry," I don't even know why I'm apologizing.

"Ten blade." He reaches out his hand, and I hand him the scalpel.

"Vascular Scissors. Is this your first time with one of theirs?" He asks me after a few minutes.

"Yes." I hand him the scissors and turn around for a moment, examining his soldier's uniform laying on the floor. According to his ranks, he is an officer.

"Needle J shape. With us, the doctors, we always send the new one." He smiles at me under his surgeon's mask, "so I had no choice."

"I volunteered," I hand him the needle.

"You have a grace, even though they're not going to like you for that."

But I don't answer back, and he continues to operate quietly. Maybe I was wrong that I agreed to do this, but I had no idea, and no one had told me. What other choice did I have? I have to stay focused; this is my chance to be a nurse again.

"Should I give him more morphine?" I ask the doctor when he makes another incision, and the injured soldier sighs in pain.

"No, one dose is enough for him. We should keep the morphine for the rest of our wounded. I'm done." He looks up at me, "you can take it from here; continue closing to finish the job. Use the curved needle." He hands me the scalpels and backs away from the wounded soldier, cursing under his breath before getting out of the room. I'm left alone with the German wounded soldier lying on the operating table.

My fingers tremble as I try to prepare the thread to suture his wounds. It's been a long time since the last time I stitched an injury, and I have to hurry so that the wound doesn't get infected. But my eyes constantly wander from his pale chest to the floor, where his boots lay next to his torn German

Air Force uniform. His eyes are closed, and his face is still covered with dirt and soot from a fire; a sign of him escaping a burning plane. Why did they bring him to us? Couldn't they just leave him exactly where they had found him?

I stop the suturing for a moment, take a clean bandage, wet it with some water, and clean the remnants of blood and soot from his face, feeling his skin and warm lips. He is still alive. I have to keep sewing him back up.

My fingers quickly run over his open wound, closing it as I try to ignore his uniform and boots staring at me from the floor. When I finally can't take it any longer, I kick them with my healthy leg, holding the operating table for support. Why did they ask me to treat him?

"I'm done," I call out into the hall after a few minutes. I make sure to wash my hands thoroughly, and go out into the hallway, looking for the soldiers who can take him wherever they take wounded like him.

"Can we take him?" Two soldiers approach us and hold his arms and legs, transferring him to a hospital bed.

"Carefully, where are you taking him?"

"To the end of the hall, behind the curtain, he should be separated from the rest of the wounded. Head Nurse Blanche said there are two wounded in recovery there, who need to be moved."

***

What do I tell John? I have no courage to help them move him to a new place.

I stand at the entrance of the hall and see the soldiers waiting patiently, standing by the German's bed, while Audrey approaches John, strokes his arm, and explains something to him. I'm not sure he understands.

What have I done? Now he will be even more alone. Why did I agree to help with the surgery?

John gets up from his bed and walks beside her, holding the metal frame of the bed as she pushes it to another spot in the hall. Someone else takes my bed and moves it along the aisle, placing it in another corner, far away from John.

The wounded German remains in the spot that was once ours; with the two soldiers standing on either side of him. I keep looking at them until one of them pulls the curtain closed obstructing my view. I need to go and get used to the new spot where my bed now stands., Maybe there's a wall I can stare at night, or another wounded soldier I can read a book to. Why do I care? It's not my job to help John recover.

"Grace?"

"Yes." I turn around towards the nurse calling me.

"Head Nurse Blanche wants to see you."

"I'm coming," I answer, but remain standing at the entrance of the hall for a few moments. This is the first time I have been invited to her office.

***

"It's good to see you walking in here without bursting." She raises her head while sitting behind her desk, looking at me.

"Yes, Head Nurse Blanche." I look at her and smile.

"Tell me, Grace, do you know anything about American army meat cans going around in the village?"

"No, Head Nurse Blanche." I lift my chin and look out of the window behind her back overlooking the bay. Even though I know she could punish me, I would have done it again if I had to.

"The surgeon said you did an excellent job."

"Thank you, Head Nurse Blanche."

"Let me tell you what we'll do until your ship arrives," she looks down at the paper lying on the table in front of her and then looks up at me again, as if expecting me to say something. I just stand there, not saying a word. Either way, she hates me already.

"We had to put the wounded German in your spot in the hall," she says what I already know, ignoring the fact that I don't have my little corner anymore. "He's a prisoner of war." She carries on, "he should be separated from the other wounded. You can take your things and go find yourself an empty bed in one of the nurses' rooms."

"Thank you, Head Nurse Blanche." It takes me a second to register what she is saying to me, but I keep standing still.

"And make sure they give you a new white nurses' uniform." She holds a rubber stamp and presses it against the paper lying in front of her, handing it to me. "Here, this time you will have the right note of request."

"Yes, Head Nurse Blanche." I'm not daring to smile; afraid she might change her mind.

"And get out of my office so you can start celebrating, now that you've finally got what you wanted. Luckily for you, I have a shortage of nurses."

"Yes, Head Nurse Blanche."

I close the door behind me and lean against it. I succeeded. My hand is holding the note instructing them to give me a new uniform. I must tell John; he will be so pleased with me. I have so much to organize. Perhaps I'll invite him to dance with me again on the road tonight. I don't care if my leg hurts. I close my eyes and smile to myself. I'll tell him right away.

"John, hold on to me." I see Audrey leading him out of the hall toward the garden, guiding him to place his hand on her shoulder as they slowly walk out.

"Let's go outside. I'll lead you to the bench and come back to visit you later." She smiles at me when she notices me standing at the top of the stairs.

"Yes, Nurse Audrey, I like to sit outside and look at the sea." He answers her, and I cringe. How can I tell him I will no longer be by his side? Who will read to him every night?

My eyes follow them as they leave the hall and walk towards the garden, careful not to move or make any noise, thinking how lucky it is that he can't see.

After they disappear into the garden and I can't hear them anymore, I go down the stairs of the second floor and into the hall, limping to the corner that was once ours. I must take my things out of the locker; this is the German's spot now.

I count thirty-eight steps as I look

around at the wounded, occasionally looking at the floor and being careful not to slip; my corner is waiting for me one last time.

The wounded German is lying in the spot that was previously mine, his eyes are closed, and his pale chest moves slowly with each breath he takes. The locker that John and I shared is by his side now, still filled with my personal belongings. The soldiers who had accompanied him disappeared, and he looked just like any other wounded soldier covered with bandages.

"Goodbye, wall," I whisper to my loyal wall, running my hand over it for the last time, pressing my fingers against the lines that counted the days of the approaching ship, looking at the drawings I had made and touching the peeling plaster that I had removed with my nails when I was in so much pain. "Thanks."

I bend over to the metal locker, pulling out my army duffel bag and small personal backpack, the only item that came with me to the hospital after the injury. All of my other equipment was lost. One last look to see if I had forgotten anything behind me, and I turn to walk away.

For a moment, I look at the German, thinking that not so long ago I was lying there, just like him. I managed to move forward; this is no longer my place. Suddenly, this corner of the hall and the man breathing quietly seem foreign to me; I have to get out of there and go to my new room.

An hour later, I place my bag on the empty bed in the nurses' room on the second floor. This is my spot from now on. All of the other nurses are on duty; I look at their iron beds covered with military wool blankets. I put the new white uniform I received right beside the khaki ones, folded on the bed.

Button after button, I button the white uniform up and examine myself in the filthy mirror attached to the wall. My wooden leg seems so noticeable. What can I do?

"You are Pinocchio," I whisper to myself, "you are a wooden doll who dreams of being a real child."

I sit down on the creaking iron bed and try to pull the white socks up as much as I can, but that's not enough, the yellow wooden prosthetic can be seen above them.

"Pinocchio, you will never become a real child. Your wooden leg will always stand out." I say to myself as I get up and try to pull the uniform dress down as much as possible, but it's not enough of course, everyone will be able to see that I am a wooden Pinocchio, a lame doll who struggles to walk.

I take off the white nurse's uniform and put on the simple khaki pants instead. They look like the ones I had at the hospital on the front lines. At least these ones are clean and not stained with mud and blood.

"Now I look just like a lame soldier," I whisper to myself as I look in the mirror.

"You can't tell I don't have a leg, nor that I'm a nurse." I wipe the tears from my eyes, open my personal bag, and turn its contents over on the stretched woolen blanket on the bed.

My fingers search through my things until I find two photos of myself that I had brought with me from home. The photos were taken on the day I finished nursing school. There I am, standing and smiling, both legs still attached. I hate these pictures, and I hate the leg I no longer have.

I take John's lighter, bring the yellow photos closer to the flame, and watch them burn with great satisfaction.

"Now I'm just the khaki Pinocchio, no more Grace with both legs," I whisper to the ash flakes scattered on the floor, crushing them with my wooden leg.

"Are you the new nurse, Grace?" A nurse I've never met before is standing at the door.

"Yes."

"I have been told to come get you, there's surgery, and they need you."

"I'm coming," I say to her, wiping my tears. I must stop with all this crying.

Careful not to slip, I walk into the operating room, tucking John's lighter into my pocket. I will tell him that I'm back to being a nurse in the evening.

***

I have been sitting in the dark in the garden for hours, looking at the hospital windows, waiting for everyone to go to sleep. Maybe John will fall asleep as well. I assisted in three surgeries today, working with two doctors who said I did an excellent job. Still, I hesitate to go into the building and look for John's bed and tell him that I am a nurse again.

The building windows go dark one by one until only two are left lit, looking like two eyes in the dark, staring at me. One of them probably belongs to Head Nurse Blanche, who never sleeps. I must get up and go search for his bed. I must promise him that I'll keep on coming to visit him.

In the pocket of my new uniform, there is a letter I wrote to him in between surgeries. She's telling him how much she misses their conversations. Still, I don't get up, it feels nice to keep sitting on the bench outside, all alone in the night.

Another window in the building goes dark, leaving only one to brighten up the blackness of the night outside; it's like a lighthouse showing me my way back home. It's time to go inside.

I keep sitting on the bench, playing with my cane. I asked Francesca to bring me a new one after giving John the one I had received from her as a gift.

"Americana, you do not give away my gifts, do you hear?" She said, still agreeing to bring me a new stick in exchange for a couple of canned meat and cigarettes.

"Americana, I don't need your charity." She looked at me, taking the things from my hands. "And don't think this is going to make me be nicer to you." She turned her back to me and walked to our spot behind the shed.

I take the cane she brought me from the village and use it as I slowly climb the stairs to the second floor, walking to the nurses' sleeping quarters. He must have fallen asleep already, I'll visit him tomorrow.

"Good afternoon, Gracie, I can recognize you by your walk." John says the next day as I approach and sit beside him on the bench overlooking the sea. He's never called me Gracie before, and I want to hold his hand resting on the bench, but I'm restraining myself from doing so.

"I wanted to come yesterday, but I was busy."

"It's okay, isn't it ironic?" He smiles at the sky.

"Why Ironic?" I feel sorry that I didn't come talk to him yesterday.

"Because at the end, the Germans did manage to separate between us." He looks in my direction, even though he doesn't see me.

"What did they tell you?"

"That there is a wounded German prisoner of war recovering in the hall and that he should be separated from the others."

"And that's it?" Did they tell him who helped operate on him?

"No," he moves his head and continues smiling into the horizon, "they told me that you have recovered and that I will no longer be sleeping by your side. That you have returned to being a lovely nurse wearing a white uniform. Well, they didn't actually mention the white uniform."

"Yes, I have recovered, but in the meantime, I'm staying here." I finally hold his hand resting on the bench. I won't leave him alone.

"Can you see the seagull?" He points his chin towards the horizon, and I look at the sky and the clouds in the distance but don't see a single bird.

"I'm sorry, I can't see it."

"It's because you're not blind," he smiles at me, "I can see what I want, and you look like a seagull. You're a lovely nurse in a white uniform."

"Yes, I'm a nurse wearing a white uniform." I don't want to tell him why I'm wearing the khaki pants instead of the white dress.

"It's time for you to start flying, spread your wings like a white bird." He looks in my direction, white bandages are covering his eyes.

"But I'll come visit you every day." I take the letter I had written for him out of my pocket, but after a second, I regret it and put it back. "I'll come visit you at night, I promise."

"You won't come, but it's okay." He turns his gaze back to the sea, "We're at war, you shouldn't make promises at war, and you're like the seagull that flies one place to another."

I want to tell him that he and Georgia had made promises to each other, but then I think of her and her broken promise and stop myself.

"I'll come in the evening." I get up and walk away from him.

"Goodbye, Gracie from Chicago." I'm glad he's calling me Gracie.

"Goodbye, John from Cold Spring, New York. I'll come visit." I'm walking away from him, knowing I'm not going to keep my promise as I've already registered to assist surgeries tonight.

***

The next afternoon, after finishing my shift, I see her sitting behind the shed, in the corner that belongs to me. She's leaning against the old wall, sitting on the ground like I usually do.

"Audrey, are you okay?" I stand at a distance from her.

"I know you tend to sit here," she looks at me, "this is the secret spot where the limping nurse usually hides at, isn't it?"

I stand and look at her while she takes a box of cigarettes out of her white uniform pocket and lights one, blowing the smoke slowly, "I haven't changed his bandages in two days." She looks up at me again.

"Whose bandages?"

"His."

"The German's?"

"Yes." She nods her head and continues to speak slowly. "For two days now, I've been approaching his bed, standing behind the curtain and doing nothing."

"Why?" I look at her trembling fingers holding the cigarette.

"I know I need to change his bandages." She motions for me to sit next to her, "and that if I don't change them, he will die, and I'm a professional nurse who knows how to do her job, but I just can't take care of him."

"Yes, there is an oath nurses take, and we must uphold it." I keep standing next to her. She's not my friend.

"Gracie, you can sit down. I won't bite you." She moves a little and makes room for me, and I sit down but keep some distance from her. I hate that she calls me Gracie.

"Do you believe in this oath?" She asks me as I lean against the old wall, feeling the rough plaster through my khaki uniform.

"I don't know." My hands play with the dry leaves scattered around me.

"I believe in this oath, that we should take care of all wounded, no matter what," she exhales the smoke, "and I'm a professional nurse." She continues to speak slowly, "but I'm standing and looking at him, unable to touch him. He's German."

"You know," she continues after a moment, not waiting for me to answer, "when they brought him in, Blanche specifically called me to her office and asked if I would be willing to take care of him because none of the other nurses are willing to do that. She told me that I'm the only one she can count on. I'm always the one that can be relied upon, even when it comes to taking care of a screaming intern nurse, who has lost her leg." She blows the smoke into the sky again and looks at me, but I lower my eyes.

"Thank you," I say after a time.

"And I told her I was ready," She ignores my 'thank you,' "because I'm a professional nurse and he's a wounded man just like all the other wounded. Except that he's not like the other wounded. He's German."

"Is that why you wanted me to assist during his surgery?"

"Not everything is about you, Gracie, I'm the one taking care of the German. When I stand by his bed and look at him, I can't stop thinking that maybe he's the pilot who shot at us that day?" Her fingers play with the leaves scattered around us, crumbling one of them.

"I don't think he's one of them," I answer, "there are far too many German pilots in the sky for it to be him."

"So maybe it's some of his friends? So why should we take care of him? Why does he deserve to live? Maybe he deserves to die?"

"I don't know," I answer her. What

can I tell her? That she must treat him? That she took an oath? Does anyone even listen to the oaths and the promises in this never-ending war?

"You're probably one of those people who wanted to save the world, just like the woman at the recruiting center promised you would." She looks at me, and I smile a bitter smile back at her, remembering the woman at the recruiting center and the words she said.

"Girls, when you travel overseas, your white uniform represents the good, compassionate America, the one that extends a supportive hand to the Americans wounded and all of the wounded who are fighting in this difficult war." She spoke enthusiastically, then, at the recruitment conference in Chicago.

"Yes, I wanted to save the world," I answer her.

"I came here to be a professional, and I'm a professional nurse. For two years now, I've been a professional, tidy nurse, working according to the rules, smiling at the wounded, caring for them, stroking their hair." She doesn't look at me when she speaks, "I'm good to everyone, but suddenly there's this German."

I don't reply, I just keep playing with the dry leaves on the ground. What can I tell her to encourage her? Even though she treated me, she doesn't really like me. She used to like me only when I was helpless.

"But not with him," she continues, "Gracie, I think I shouldn't take care of him, you know." She looks at me again, "I stand by his bed and look at him and think maybe he should die. Maybe it's time for another nurse to take care of him. I shouldn't be taking care of the German, and it doesn't make me any less good of a nurse."

"No, it doesn't make you any less good of a nurse," I answer her and light a cigarette for myself, exhaling the smoke, looking up at the cloudy sky.

***

"Do you speak any German?" I ask Francesca when she comes in from the village the following day. She gets off her noisy motorcycle and covers it with a tarp to protect it from the dripping rain. It's been raining since morning.

"I won't help you." She answers me and starts walking towards the hospital entrance.

"You didn't even hear what I need from you."

"I know exactly what you need," she stands in front of me, her wild hair wet from the rain. "You need someone to help you with the German soldier because none of you speak German, so they sent you to try and talk to the cursing Italian and convince her to help you."

"Francesca, please, I need help." I try to keep up with her as she walks towards the hospital, but I'm having a hard time walking on the wet gravel.

"You don't need help. He needs help." She stops and looks at me angrily, "And yes, I know German, but no, I won't help him." She turns her back to me and walks towards the building.

"I'm the one taking care of him." I shout after her.

She stops suddenly, turns around, and comes back towards me even though the rain keeps getting stronger and we're both getting wet now. "I'll tell you what you're taking care of," she stands in front of me, "you're taking care of a German soldier."

"I know."

"No, you don't know, you don't know anything!" She continues. "Do you remember the destroyed tank at the entrance to the village, the one the kids always play on top of?"

"Yes," I say quietly, wiping the raindrops off my cheeks.

"At first, they were nice because we were on their side. They would even stop in the village sometimes, get down from their armored vehicles and buy groceries, paying with German reichsmarks. The wounded German is nice now, whispering danke every time you change his bandages. But when the Americans, started approaching, they became less nice." She pauses and breathes, "Then they started planting land mines on the roads, and in various places in the village. Believe me, it's a lot less nice. One of those mines hit and burned the American tank at the entrance of the village. A German gift."

"I didn't know," I whisper to her.

"You know nothing, Americana." She looks at me. "It took your soldiers weeks to locate the mines. And there were many injured people in the meantime. Who do you think treated them? We had no doctors left in the village. The only ones left were the old men. The fascists and the Germans took all the young men into their army by force; they took the doctors too. We didn't have any doctors to treat the wounded. And we definitely didn't have a magnificent hospital like you do now." She keeps on talking.

"I'm sorry."

"You know," she ignores my apology, "have you ever asked yourself why the children in the village love you so much?"

"Why?" I wipe the rain off my cheeks again, noticing that my whole body is wet.

"They think that you are a fairy, since you were wounded and survived, they think you must have some kind of magical powers. Because, in our village, after the Germans had left their presents, no one survived their injuries." She smiles at me a little, and I smile back at her.

"Do you understand? When the Germans left, I spat in their direction and went to church, praying that they would never come back. Then suddenly I see a convoy of German prisoner soldiers marching on the road from my village, followed by this wounded German pilot. What if tomorrow the Americans decide to withdraw their forces from Italy, or my village, and retreat? What would happen to us if the Germans return?"

"We will not withdraw," I answer her. I really hope I'm right.

"Yes, for an Americana who knows nothing, you sure are very confident." She turns her back to me again and starts walking towards the entrance of the hospital, soaking wet from the rain.

"I know I shouldn't take care of him." I yell at her, "and I know he deserves to die." She stops but doesn't turn back to face me.

"And I know you hate me too." I keep talking to her, "but every time I change his bandages, I think of your husband. Maybe he's in a Russian prison camp, lying in a bed wounded, while a Russian nurse changes his bandage and takes care of him, keeping him alive." I wipe my wet face.

"Don't bring my husband into this," she turns to me again and shouts.

"Maybe I'm naive," I reply to her, "but it gives me something to believe in, and maybe it's a small thing, but sometimes small is better than nothing."

"You're not taking care of him for me, you're taking care of him for you. You're willing to do anything so that everyone would see you as a nurse again." She shouts and turns her back towards me one last time, entering the building, leaving me soaking in the rain.

***

"Danke," he sighs and whispers to me after I finish changing his bandages, generously spreading sulfa powder on his fair skin so that his injury won't get infected. Sometimes I think of dressing his wound without the disinfectant or putting only a small amount of it. But I try to banish this sort of thoughts from my head, focusing on my movements: cutting, removing, cleaning, spreading sulfa powder, and dressing the wound again.

He tries not to moan in pain, even though I know that it hurts him. Perhaps he knows that all the other wounded in the hall are staring at him from behind the curtain, wishing him dead. I was even instructed not to give him any morphine; it should be saved for our own wounded.

Sometimes, I stay standing next to him quietly in the corner where my bed once stood, watching him sleep, not wanting to go out and deal with the hateful stares of the other wounded. Those stares always accompany me outside as I pass in the aisle.

How does it feel to fly? I hold the iron frame of his hospital bed, close my eyes, and imagine my fingers gripping the control stick of an airplane. I never flew.

How does it feel when the engines roar, and the airplane lifts off from the ground? I open my eyes and look at him. He has light, short hair, and his bright face was unharmed in the plane crash. He's about my age.

What does it feel like to look through your airplane scope and engage the trigger that shoots streams of bullets at people? I once saw it in a news diary playing before a movie back home, in America. The pilot smiled at the camera as the announcer explained in an enthusiastic voice how our heroic pilots fire their machineguns at the enemy. How did you feel when you shot people? When you pressed the button that fired at me from the sky, did you smile too?

I open my eyes and look at his face and his light hair. He looks back at me and tries to smile. The air feels stifling here behind the curtain, I have to get out of here.

I say nothing as I cross the curtain back into the main hall, making sure to pull the curtain closed after myself. I'll come back later to see how he's doing and whether he's still alive.

Francesca stands outside the curtain as if trying to make sure that I don't talk to him or stay by his side for too long. It doesn't matter as I don't understand any German, even the few words he says as he moans. But she's not the only one that is watching me. It seems to me that all of the other soldier's eyes are staring at me as I walk across the hall, leaning on my wooden cane. As I walk by them, I keep my eyes on the floor; I must be careful not to stumble.

Knock, knock, knock, I hear the wooden stick hit the floor. I can also hear Francesca's steps right behind me. She's probably here because she wants to make sure I don't stay by his side.

Even though they're all staring at me, no one says a word, maybe due to Francesca's presence. "German lover," I heard someone whisper once as I passed by, but Francesca cursed at him, and he hasn't spoken to me since. I'll visit him again later when everyone is asleep.

"Meine uniformen." He sighs and whispers to me the next time I come to check his wound, trying not to hurt him.

Before I came to see him, I thought about giving him a dose of morphine. This would have involved taking one syringe from the nurses' station and hiding it. But I couldn't do it. Was he a fighter pilot or a bomber pilot? Does it matter at all?

"Meine uniformen." He whispers again and looks at me in the dim light of the lamp that is still on. I don't answer him. I don't want to talk to him. He's my enemy, and I don't want to see his human side.

"He wants his uniform," I hear Francesca. She stands in the corner, leaning against the wall, watching me, checking my every move.

"Why does he need his uniform?" I turn to her.

"He probably wants to wear it again and be a proud German soldier." She answers and crosses her arms over her chest. "I'm not going to ask him. He's your wounded German." She goes away, forcibly closing the curtain behind her.

"Meine Uniformen." He whispers to

me again. How many people did he kill while wearing his uniform?

"Where are you going?" Francesca asks me, following me as I walk through the hall.

"That's none of your business," I answer her, but she keeps on following me.

"You're looking for the German's uniform."

"That's none of your business." I go down the stairs, holding on to the railing, careful not to stumble.

"Are you actually trying to help him?" She walks after me to the back of the building, standing behind me as I start rummaging through the piles of torn uniforms tossed near the trash cans.

"I don't know," I answer her.

"Yes, I forgot, you're an Americana who knows nothing."

I don't answer her. She doesn't have to help me if she doesn't want to.

Finally, my hands pull his torn gray-blue uniform out of the dirty pile. I look at it, examining it carefully. Why did he mention his uniform?

On the uniform, I see his officers' ranks. I rip off the epaulets, and throw them back into the torn uniforms pile. I do the same with all of his war medals; he probably received them for killing American soldiers. My fingers open the buttoned pockets and search through them.

"I thought you wanted to give him his ranks back." I hear Francesca.

"I despise his ranks and what they represent." My fingers keep searching the shirt pockets.

I find a packet with a drawing of a German eagle and the word 'chocolate' written above it, and offer it to Francesca, but she looks at the eagle holding the swastika with its claws and throws it angrily back into the pile of dirty uniforms, looking at it with contempt. There is a holster of a pistol without the pistol, probably taken by those who got to him first, and a wallet. My fingers pull out some German banknotes, a military certificate with his name, 'Herald,' and a photo of a girl with golden curly hair.

The back of the photo reads "Elke, Summer 1942." Francesca looks at the photo without saying a word. She doesn't say anything even as

I return to the German's bed and place the photo in his hand. He looks at the picture for a moment and whispers, "Danke," turning his gaze back to the wall, his bandaged chest rising and falling gently with each breath.

I rush out closing the curtain behind me again and walk away looking at the floor. At least John can't see me, otherwise he might end up hating me like the rest of them. I haven't visited him at night since I started working as a nurse again, but I can't be thinking about that right now, I have a wounded German to care of.

***

Several days later, I pull the curtain that hides the German back, holding a packet of clean bandages and a jar of sulfa powder, but his bed is empty.

The German pilot no longer lies in his bed, and any trace of his existence has disappeared. The bottle of iodine I left on the locker next to the bed last night was also taken, as was the newspaper someone had left for him, the headline reading: "The German army has withdrawn from Belgium." What happened to him? Did he not survive the night?

I close the curtain behind me, not wanting to be exposed to the other wounded who are watching me, holding the hospital bed frame, taking a deep breath. Maybe it's better that he's not here anymore.

My hand searches through the bed sheets, but the picture of the girl I gave him a few days ago has also disappeared.

"The German, where is he?" I walk to the nurses' station, take the patients' list, and go through it, looking for his name, but he's not on the list anymore.

"Good morning, Gracie." Audrey smiles at me, "I was wondering when you would notice that the wounded soldier you were responsible for no longer exists."

"The German wounded, where is he?"

"I thought you would be interested to know what happened to him." She looks at me with her red lips.

"What happened to him?"

"He ended up going to the right place for enemies like him."

"Did he pass away last night?"

"Unfortunately, no." She goes back to the newspaper she is reading, "they came and took him to a POW camp. They decided that he recovered enough to be sleeping behind barbed wire."

I look at her and think whether to ask her who took him and which POW camp they took him to, but I decide to say nothing. She's right, that is the right place for him. He's a German pilot who killed American soldiers. Even if he has a face, a name and a woman who's waiting for him at home, he's still my enemy, and I shouldn't think about him anymore. I must be just like Audrey, believing he deserves to die, and maybe everyone would forgive me for keeping him alive.

"You can always go visit him there." She continues to talk to me without raising her head from the newspaper, "I'm sure he will be very happy if you do."

"Yes, I'm sure you'd be happy too. Nothing can stop you from being a professional nurse who takes care of all of the wounded in this hospital," I tell her and walk away, not waiting to hear what she has to say to me. I should go ask John if he wants me to take him back to his previous spot.

***

"Grace?" He turns to me as I approach him, hearing my cane hitting the floor.

"Yes, it's me." I hate that he recognizes me by my walk. "How are you?" I approach and stand by his bed.

"You should meet Edward. He is the wounded man lying next to me," John extends his hand in the air, aiming to the bed beside him, "I have to admit that Edward doesn't read as nice as you do; he should really work on his reading tone." And I look at Edward, who is smiling at me, and reply with a polite smile.

"I'm happy to hear that." I get closer to John and lay my hand on his bed.

"He also agreed to keep reading

right where you left off from, even though he didn't know the beginning."

"Luckily, I have dog-ears all over the book," I say to John, want to stroke his hair, ask him how he feels.

"He's one of those old-school people who claim we shouldn't dog-ear books. He insists that it destroys them."

"I promise to stop destroying books." I smile at Edward and remember all the times this book had been thrown on the floor in the recent months, "I was thinking of reading you a little."

"That's nice of you, but there is no need. I'll continue reading with Edward later." He said, as I removed my hand from his bed. I wanted to sit close to him and give my foot some rest, but now it seemed inappropriate.

"Our corner at the end of the hall has become available again. I thought you might want to go back there."

"No, thank you, it's nice for me to be here together with everyone around. They treat me very well." Edward smiles at me again.

"We promise to take care of him and thank you for the book, even though you're tend to ruin books with your dog-ears." He says.

"You're welcome," I reply and begin to walk away, thinking of all the things I have ruined. "Bye John, I'll come visit again soon."

"Goodbye, Grace. It was nice to meet you." Edward waves his hand at me.

"Goodbye, Grace." John waves his hand as well. He could have asked me to stay longer. He could have also call me Gracie.

***

Although it's not my job, I go back to the corner of the hall to make the German's bed.

My fingers check between the sheets to see whether he had forgotten something, but he took everything with him. There is nothing on the floor or in the locker, no memory of anyone ever sleeping there; neither me nor John nor Herald the German.

For a moment, I am tempted to lie on the bed and look at the wall, as I have done so many times before. For a few minutes, I want to go back to the time when this place was my home. But I know that things have changed, I'm already wearing a nurse's uniform instead of the hospital clothes. I had made a promise to myself that I would move forward.

My fingers run over the peeled wall, feeling the plaster and the cracks still familiar to me, but then I notice there is something new there.

'Herald war hier 1944.' Someone had engraved the letters on the wall with a sharp object. As I approach and touch the letters with my fingers, feeling the grooves, I notice the writing below, in smaller letters: 'Danke Grace, Danke Italiana.'

I sit on the bed for a few minutes and lie down on the white sheets, looking at the ceiling. I don't care if any of the wounded or the nurses see me now. I don't care if they talk about me, they hate me either way.

"Were you taking care of him as well?" I ask after finding her in the garden, leaning against the shed wall.

She sits and smokes, looking at the autumn sky without answering me.

"Were you taking care of him as well?" I ask her again and sit down next to her.

"It has nothing to do with you, Americana," she says at last, looking at the sky and returning to her silence.

But after a few moments, she speaks again, whispering to herself. "Maybe it has something to do with me hoping that there might be someone in Russia who is taking care of my husband if he's lying there injured."

I hold her hand, feeling the warmth of her fingers.

***

Several days later, I can feel the pleasant afternoon sun as I turn onto the main road and head back to the hospital. I must practice walking without my cane, even though my leg hurts.

I slowly pass the broken gate, enter the front driveway, and turn around to make a detour behind the parking trucks to the garden at the back of the hospital. Today, like all days, they sit on the steps at the entrance talking to each other.

"Hi, German lover, come join us." Audrey waves and signs for me to come closer.

I ignore her and keep on walking, pretending that I didn't hear her, but another nurse calls my name, and I stop and approach them.

"Come, sit with us," one of the nurses moves a little, making room for me on the white stairs. I think it's the nurse who helped me then with the list. I bend down carefully and sit between them, and they all look at me as if I were an exotic animal that escaped the zoo.

"Weren't you afraid of him?" One of them finally asks.

"The German?"

"Yes."

"No, I wasn't afraid. He was injured." He was also in pain, like our other wounded, I think to myself.

"And how did you feel? Didn't it bother you that you were taking care of the enemy?" Someone else asks me.

"I didn't think about it." I turn to her, wanting to tell her how hard I tried not to think about whether he likes Hitler or not, or whether he was drafted into the army by force. I want to tell them how hard it was not to think about whether he likes to kill American pilots, or was he scared when he got into his plane every morning. But I'm not sure they would understand me if I told them all of my thoughts and fears. I'm not sure I understand myself either.

"And you just volunteered to take care of him?" She asks me, and I look at Audrey, who lowers her eyes.

"No, I was asked to do that," I answer her and look at Audrey's red lips, "Head Nurse Blanche asked me."

"You're kind." The nurse smiles at me.

"Thanks." I smile back at her and look at Audrey.

"Would you mind it if he died?" Audrey joins the talking. What should I answer her?

"I don't know," I look at her, "I just know that I'm no longer the same Grace who boarded the ship in New York Harbor almost a year ago."

"It's because you have no leg." She laughs, and I look down, struggling to keep myself from getting up and walking away.

"I'm also not the same person I used to be before I arrived here." Says one of the nurses, "I helped so many soldiers, and I saved lives, but I saw things I shouldn't have seen, and sometimes I don't know if it was a clever idea to get on the ship that brought me here or maybe I should have run away."

"Me too," says another nurse.

"Luckily, the German was transferred to a POW camp. At least he won't be able to kill anymore," Audrey says, and another nurse nods in agreement.

"Grace," one of the nurses turns to me, "you're one of us now. You're a nurse, aren't you? You should come with us to visit the pilots at their club."

"She's an intern nurse," Audrey replies, "and besides, how will she come with us wearing those khaki uniforms she's wearing while limping? Why would anyone even look at her?"

***

End of Part 1

Made in the USA
Middletown, DE
11 August 2023

36591644R00245